Cover Copy

There can be only one…for both of them.

Sent back in time to the year 1210 when their Highlander shifter clan first began, three identical brothers known as the 'power of three' must find their mates if they wish to save their future line from extinction.

Fae-blooded Arabel holds the deadly and rare fire-wielder skill, an ability that flares beyond her control when her shifter mate travels to the past and begins closing in on her. Unable to allow an intimacy with him for fear she'll bring about his death, she enlists the aid of one of her fae kind to compel him, so that no matter how many times they might meet, each instance will be as if the first and all other times forgotten.

Highland warrior shifter Finlay Matheson is on a mission to find his mate and each time he meets Arabel, he falls inescapably in love. If only he didn't keep forgetting her each time they parted ways. Determined and unwavering in his mission, when he is called to save Arabel's village from being destroyed by her enemy, he races to aid and protect her.

Battling both love and land, Finlay must find a way for them to be together…and without perishing when they do.

Books by Joanne Wadsworth

The Matheson Brothers Series
Highlander's Desire, Book One
Highlander's Passion, Book Two
Highlander's Seduction, Book Three
Highlander's Kiss, Book Four
Highlander's Heart, Book Five
Highlander's Sword, Book Six
Highlander's Bride, Book Seven
Highlander's Caress, Book Eight
Highlander's Touch, Book Nine
Highlander's Shifter, Book Ten
Highlander's Claim, Book Eleven
Highlander's Courage, Book Twelve
Highlander's Mermaid, Book Thirteen

Highlander Heat Series
Highlander's Castle, Book One
Highlander's Magic, Book Two
Highlander's Charm, Book Three
Highlander's Guardian, Book Four
Highlander's Faerie, Book Five
Highlander's Champion, Book Six
Highlander's Captive (Short Story)

Billionaire Bodyguards Series
Billionaire Bodyguard Attraction, Book One
Billionaire Bodyguard Boss, Book Two
Billionaire Bodyguard Fling, Book Three

Books by Joanne Wadsworth

Regency Brides Series
The Duke's Bride, Book One
The Earl's Bride, Book Two
The Wartime Bride, Book Three
The Earl's Secret Bride, Book Four
The Prince's Bride, Book Five
Her Pirate Prince, Book Six

Princesses of Myth Series
Protector, Book One
Warrior, Book Two
Hunter (Short Story - Included in Warrior, Book Two)
Enchanter, Book Three
Healer, Book Four
Chaser, Book Five

Highlander's Passion

The Matheson Brothers, Book Two

JOANNE WADSWORTH

Acknowledgements

I have an incredibly supportive family who allow me so much time to write. Huge thanks go to my hubby, Jason, and kiddies, Marisa, Caleb, Cruise and Rocco. Hugs.

For my readers, I can't thank you enough for joining me, and taking this journey to where imagination and magic soar.

Gilleoin – The Legend

In the twelfth century, a man named Gilleoin became the first and only known man to hold bear shifter blood, an ability gifted to him by The Most High One. His clan was called Matheson, and when he mated with a woman carrying faerie blood, they created a line shrouded in secrecy, a line that far into the future, now neared extinction…

The Seer – Nessa

The ancient House of Clan Matheson, led by Gilleoin, the Chief of Clan Matheson, Scotland, 1210.

As the midnight hour struck, Nessa, her clan's fae-blooded seer, crossed the darkened inner courtyard toward the gate, her black fur cloak secured tight over her shoulders. Torches mounted on the stone walls spread their flickering glow across the stony ground and up along the battlements where double the number of guardsmen stood on duty in battle attire, their claymores holstered at their sides.

Restless after all that had transpired this eve, she hastened her step and passed through the arched gate then traversed down the winding trail toward Loch Alsh which reflected the beauty of moon's glow on its white-capped waves.

On a fallen log, she perched and slowly bowed her head. So many thoughts consumed her mind. A seer's life was never easy and she'd been gifted with a skill she upheld to the best of her ability, although none other than a seer could have ever foreseen the terrible battle about to ensue. Their enemy, the Chief of MacKenzie, would soon strike at their very heart and blood would flow within the village nestled farther along the loch. Some of the villagers, those directly descended from the faerie prince who'd wed their chief's daughter two centuries past, held a touch of fae blood and as such also held rare and divine skills. Never would she allow her fae kind to be harmed, and thankfully earlier this eve she'd received aid in her mission, help that had miraculously come from another time and place.

Three identical warrior brothers of immense strength—Iain, Finlay, and Kirk—had traveled through a portal from the future into her time, three men who could shift shape into the form of the bear. They could draw claws and roar as Gilleoin and his two sons could. These three warriors, known as the 'power of three,' had also arrived with Iain's mate, Isla, a fae-blooded shifter from the future, the daughter of Murdock, her clan's chief and seer.

Over the years and the centuries separating them, Nessa had come to know Murdock through joint visions. They held the same beliefs and goals, although unfortunately in the future where he lived, Gilleoin's shifter clan now neared extinction and required a new infusion of fae blood within their shifter line, an infusion she needed to make certain occurred.

Eyes closed, Nessa once again searched deep within her mind. Visions couldn't be forced, but with this level of worry and anxiety rolling through her, it usually meant one was close to rising. Images teased the periphery of her mind and she grasped ahold of them.

Her granddaughter hurried through the forest nearby, her fae skill of fire flaring beyond her control, each step she took scorching the earth underfoot. Arabel raced toward an icy pool of water, fell to her knees at the edge and plunged her hands into the cool depths. Steam billowed into the air, and she slumped forward, her shoulders heaving as she gulped deep breaths.

Nessa's sight swirled again with another barrage of images, her second vision coming hard on the heels of her first. Finlay, one of the three brothers who'd arrived from the future, jogged through the postern gate on the other side of the castle then dropped to all fours, and in a sizzling display made the Change. One massive bear with silky black fur lumbered into the woods, his beast restless as he pawed the ground then rose up on his hind legs and roared. His thunderous growl stated his frustration, that he searched for his mate and he wouldn't leave this place until he'd found her.

For five long years Iain, Finlay, and Kirk had been searching for their chosen ones in the future. Iain had found Isla recently, but Finlay and Kirk's search could only now truly begin, their women residing here in this time. Both brothers were now far closer to finding their mates than ever before, and all here wished to aid them.

With care, she returned her focus to Arabel. Her granddaughter still knelt at the pool's edge in a cloud of steam, a sense of loss and frustration rolling through her.

"Why is this happening to me?" Arabel whispered into the dead of the night. "I've never lost control for no reason afore."

Nessa would need to keep a close eye on Arabel. Not all was as it seemed, and that knowledge reverberated strongly through her. Aye, as she always would, she'd watch over each and every one of her kin, including the newcomers who'd arrived from the future. None of them need ever face their difficulties alone, not when she remained close by.

The Seer – Murdock Matheson

Matheson Castle, led by Murdock Matheson, the Chief of Clan Matheson, a man with dual shifter-fae blood, Scotland, current day.

Alone in the misty moonlight, Murdock Matheson paced the battlements overlooking the night-shrouded waters of Loch Alsh. Either side of the castle, the forest stretched for miles upon miles, providing their shifter-fae skilled clan descended from Gilleoin's firstborn son's line with the perfect level of isolation they needed from the rest of the world. As the seer and chief of his clan, he kept a constant eye on his daughter, Isla, as well as the three warrior brothers known as the 'power of three' who'd traveled through time with her to the year twelve-hundred and ten.

His daughter now resided over eight-hundred years in the past, and although he couldn't speak to her, he still sensed her closeness even over the wide chasm of time. So too Iain would never allow Isla far from his side, not now they'd finally found each other and completed their mated bond.

Aye, what a mission they all now had ahead of them. Finlay and Kirk now searched for their chosen ones, a mission of untold danger as the coming battle with the MacKenzie loomed. Hell, he desperately wished he could aid his kin in saving their fae people, although glad he was for Nessa. The seer of ancient times would watch over them all, of that he had no doubt.

Gripping the thick stone crenellation, he brought Nessa's image to the forefront of his mind. Visions came as and when they pleased, but he sensed one was close. With his eyes closed, Nessa's image fully crystalized. She sat on a fallen log under a midnight moon before the very loch he too stood before, although so many centuries past. Her head was bowed and a black fur cloak covered her shoulders, a vision cloaking her mind. At times, if the same vision assailed them, they could tap into each other's thoughts and speak across time.

With focus, he drew his attention on his ability and the vision Nessa was under. A half mile from Nessa, a young woman with long blond tresses knelt at the edge of an icy pool of water, her hands submerged within the cool depths and steam puffing into the air. A fire-wielder. The steam signified her attempt to cool herself, and her frustration and loss of control pervaded the air. Something was amiss.

He returned his focus to Nessa and whispered to her across time, "Nessa, I've caught images of the fire-wielder losing control of her skill. Who is she?"

"Murdock, 'tis good to speak to you again. The fire-wielder is my granddaughter, Arabel. The lass rarely loses control of her skill, and only if her emotions swing too widely, although we've certainly experienced quite the upheaval this eve with the arrival of the newcomers."

"Is there anything more I can do to aid you?"

"If there is, I shall let you know." The care and concern in her voice shimmered through. "Murdock, Finlay's bear rides him hard. He is desperate to find his mate."

"The war approaches and he fears losing her in the coming battle, before he's even had the chance to find her. The fae village must be saved, Nessa, so that we might once again have hope.

Gilleoin's future shifter line must survive."

"Aye, I will keep a watchful eye over all. 'Tis time to right the wrongs of the past, and this is our chance." Nessa touched her heart. "Until we speak again, my friend."

"Aye, take care." He touched his heart in return.

Nessa's image slowly fluttered away and he opened his eyes and released his grip on the rough stone crenellation. Farther along Loch Alsh, where the village had once stood, a sacred memorial standing stone tormented him with its solitary starkness. The loss of his fae kind within the village had been a burden that had consumed him for years, as it had Nessa. The unjust death of the villagers could be no more. Aye, the time to save their people had arrived and clan Matheson must once again rise to its greatest strength. The "Son of the Bear," couldn't be allowed to falter.

Chapter 1

Near the ancient House of Clan Matheson, Scotland, 1210, four days following.

Arabel's skin heated as the fire she held deep within her body raged again for release, now a fourth night in a row. She hurried along the forest trail near the castle with her twin sister at her side and emerged before a pool of water encircled by towering pine trees. Moonlight beamed through the thick foliage overhead and lit the loch's dark, glassy surface. "Thank you for coming with me, Julia," she breathed in a rush.

"Should you ever have need of me, I'll always be here."

"I'll need to fully submerge myself this eve. My heat flares too greatly to simply dunk my hands in." She turned around and gave her sister her back. "Be careful as you unlace my gown."

"Of course." Julia stepped in behind her and worked the laces loose. "Oh, you are so very, very hot. Why is this happening now?"

"I wish I knew, as well as why my very soul aches as if I've lost someone important."

"We might very well lose those we love if the MacKenzie isnae stopped." Julia wiped her brow as she stepped back. "Please, you must cool yourself. These flares must stop."

"If only there were others with my skill I could go to for guidance." She was the only one of her fire-wielder kind left, hers one of the rarest of their kind's skills. Swiftly, she shoved the long sleeves of her gown down then wriggled her hips. The soft layers of burgundy fabric slithered down her legs and swished to her feet. Grasping the folds of her ankle-length shift, she jumped out of the puddle of velvet and dashed across the damp, mossy ground and scrambled onto a large boulder.

The loch deep within the forest, small, private and perfectly round, beckoned with the promise of its cool depths within and its ability to bring her heat back down. With one deep breath, she leapt and down she went, the blessedly cool water closing in over her head. Bubbles fizzed around her, and in the murky dark, she kicked upward and emerged. Steam billowed all around, so thick her sister on the grassy bank became shrouded in the dense cloud that plumed. Treading water, she called out, "Are you all right, Julia?"

"I am. What of you?" Julia flapped a hand through the air as she moved around the pool to a clearer spot, her cheeks rosy and red.

"The water soothes me."

"I wonder," Julia said as she plopped onto a rock in her forest-green skirts, her brow wrinkled in concentration, "if the four elements have something to do with your loss of control. Fire is one of them."

"Mmm, fire, water, air and earth."

"Your first loss of control also occurred the night the newcomers arrived, the *air* so disrupted."

"Yet the air has settled while my fire continues to rage. What are they like?" Her sister had been to the fae village over the past few days and met the travelers as she had not.

"Iain is the eldest of the three and never allows Isla far from his side, no' since she is expecting. She holds both shifter and fae blood and in the future her clan lives here, while the others come from farther across the Highlands."

"Does she hold an ability?" Her fingers still itched with heat and she waved them through the water.

"One of the strongest, the skill to compel. With her hypnotic voice alone she can command any around her. The last man at the village to hold that ability passed away five and twenty years ago. 'Tis wonderful to know it continues on."

"What of Finlay and Kirk?"

"They're causing quite the stir as they search for their mates. The lasses are all quite giddy with excitement, hoping they might be the one. So far no matches have been made." She leaned forward. "The warriors are identical in every way and 'tis almost impossible to tell them apart."

She could well understand the excitement. The mated bond was an all-consuming one any couple would wish for. "I hope they find their women soon."

"So do—" Frowning, Julia rose and narrowed her gaze. "Something's wrong. Your aura has suddenly changed."

"For the better I hope."

"Nay, it now spikes out with sharp tendrils of cold-fire blue. I've no' seen the cold-fire enter your aura since our parents passed away."

"Are you certain there is cold-fire present?" She touched her chest, the soul deep ache within her having not abated one bit. Such feelings of loss could bring her cold-fire about.

"It bleeds deeper as I speak, which I dinnae like." Julia walked toward the trail's entrance. "I'll go to Nessa for an answer."

"You're leaving right now?"

"Aye, she willnae leave our village kin during their time of need."

"I'll come with you."

"Nay, remain. I'll sail rather than take the forest path, and I'll send a guard to keep watch over you." She lifted one hand and disappeared down the trail.

Wonderful. Now her aura was changing too. She hardly needed to burden her sister or their clan with all of her problems when a deadly battle loomed.

Kicking out deeper, she sent rippling waves swelling out. The cooler water continued to wash over her, as did the soul deep ache, an endless throb she couldn't disperse. Long minutes passed as she swam back and forth.

"Are you Arabel?" A warrior rode free of the forest path, his horse snorting misty air as he hauled it to a stop.

"I am." She slowed, treaded water. "Who are you?"

"Finlay Matheson. I passed Julia along the trail. She asked me to guard you, said your fire skill had flared." He dismounted in one easy and swift move.

"There's really no need to stay. I'm fine."

"How bad are these flares you're experiencing?" He slung his horse's reins over a low branch, knotted the leather then strode toward her, his great plaid secured over his broad chest with a silver pin and belted low at his waist with a leather girdle. Midnight-black hair curled onto his shoulders and his golden gaze met hers with unwavering intensity. He had the eyes of a shifter, just as Gilleoin and his sons, Kenneth and Ivan, did. So mesmerizing.

"Naught that the cool water cannae disperse."

"I see." His biceps flexed as he palmed the hilt of his mighty sword. "I'm intrigued by your skill."

"Julia wonders if the four elements of fire, water, air and earth are involved in the flares."

"The vortex that hauled us through did so within mere minutes. The air was thick and swirling fast." He propped one booted foot on the boulder next to her discarded gown. "I can't see any heat emanating from you."

"Mayhap I've cooled sufficiently." She swam toward him

and at waist-depth, slogged through the water and joined him on the grassy bank. "Do you mind checking?"

"Not at all. Tell me what to do." He extended one hand as if wishing to take hers and she shook her head.

"Nay, you must no' touch me unless all is well." She lifted her hand and turned it palm over. "If you will, bring your palm closer to mine, but halt at the point where you feel my heat. That will give me a good indication if my fire still flares too strongly."

Slowly, he lowered his hand until it hovered a little above her own. "There's no heat that I can sense, although being a shifter, my blood runs hotter than most."

"Then touch me." Her words whispered out, and far too breathy. "I mean—"

"It's all right. I know what you mean." Grinning, he picked up one of her long golden locks and curled it around his finger. "Your hair is now dry, as is your shift, so you must be emitting some heat."

"I dry my clothing with merely a thought. I am never wet for long." She shuffled closer, drawn by the spark in his golden eyes. "Where exactly do you live in the future, Finlay?"

"I live far across the Highlands toward the east near Loch Bear. Ivan, Gilleoin's second-born son, weds Bethia and becomes chief of his own clan at Ivanson Castle. Bethia doesn't hold any fae blood, which is why Ivan's line is shifter alone as Kenneth's is not. I'm one of Ivan's direct descendants." Eyes twinkling, he caught her hand and brought her palm to his cheek. "Mmm, you feel lovely and warm, just how you're supposed to."

"Are you flirting with me?" Surprise took her. No man ever had.

"Are you aware I'm here to find my chosen one?" He kissed her fingertips.

"All the lasses are." A flare of heat pulsed from her and she jerked back and broke their contact. "Oh, my apologies. Did I burn you?"

"Not at all." He held out his hand for hers again. "Allow me to touch you."

"'Tis best I return to the water."

"Then if you're returning, so am I. That water looks heavenly." He kicked off his boots. "I've also got a very playful bear who longs for a dip, that's if you don't mind sharing that water."

"You cannae swim with me. I'm a fire-wielder. Where there is fire, there is hot water."

"I love hot water, or cold. It matters not." He knelt at the loch's edge and swept one hand through it. "This isn't hot at all, a little warm, but not hot."

"It will be far hotter if you hop in with me." Her heat had flared when he'd touched her and she didn't doubt it would do so again if he came too close. "I truly dinnae need a guard even though my sister asked you to watch over me. Your brothers must surely need you."

"I left them behind. I felt a desperate urge to return early. They'll be here first thing in the morning so for tonight, or for however long you need me, I'm yours."

"Your mate could right now be at the castle and in remaining here with me, you might miss out on meeting her." She walked backward into the water and a tiny puff of steam rose. She was still too hot, but at least she was cooling.

"Possibly, but that's not going to deter me from guarding you. I gave Julia my word I'd remain." Sword belt unstrapped, he propped his weapon against the boulder then divested himself of his wrist daggers before unpinning his kilt.

Oh goodness. He was now clothed in naught but his white tunic that fluttered against him mid-thigh. She fanned her flushed cheeks at the sight of his strongly muscled legs. Never had a man unclothed himself while she watched on. She sank lower and kicked away. "Have any within your clan ever discovered that there is no mate when you come of age?"

"There are a good dozen unmated men who've been searching for their chosen ones and have had no luck in finding them."

"What if they never find them? Or you never find yours?"

"Should that happen then I will find the strength to move on. My parents and brothers would never allow me to wander too far from my clan. They hold me to the present and always will. You appear to be a strong swimmer."

"I am."

"Good, because my bear truly does wish to play and you're the only possible playmate in sight. Catch me if you can." He dove and disappeared beneath the night-shrouded waters.

Twirling around, she searched for his shadow within the loch. There wasn't even a ripple on the surface to mark his movement or a bubble to prove he'd released even the tiniest mouthful of air. She hadn't played in the longest time and even as dangerously alluring as he was, she couldn't help but dive after him. She kicked hard as she scoured the bottom of the loch for him. He had to be down here somewhere, and her lungs were near to bursting so his surely must be too. Ah, there. A hazy streak of white. His tunic. That had to be him. She clamped a hand around his ankle and he twisted around, his hair swirling about his face as he beamed at her. Then he wrapped his arms around her waist and kicked them both upward. They emerged in a burst of bubbles and she gulped in air. "I didnae realize you intended to swim at the bottom of the pool."

"I had to test your strength." He tightened his hold on her, kicking for them both. "You don't seem hot at all to me."

"Hold onto me any longer and I will surely burn you." She slipped out of his arms, tossed her feet in the air and went under. As she kicked across to the far side of the pool, a heated wave rippled out from her. His touch had her emotions rising and her excitement building. Never had she played with a man in this way before. 'Twas delightful, naughty even. Underwater, she swam then surfaced when she made the boulders bordering the far side. Clambering onto the closest one, she made it just in time as Finlay shot to the surface in a spray before her.

Grinning, he shook his dark head and sent drops flying. "So that's how you intend to play, is it?"

"You are very slow under the water." She shoved a wave of water at him and giggled. "Show me your bear, Finlay, since you insist he's the one who wishes to play."

"My bear's in a desperate mood to Change, so you're about to get your wish." He gripped the hem of his tunic under the water and held still. "The shirt has to go though. I detest shredding my clothing. Close your eyes if you need to."

She should, but for the life of her she couldn't.

"Last chance." Challenge glimmered in his eyes, a dare she couldn't help but meet.

"Go right ahead."

"As you wish." He hauled his wet tunic over his head and tossed it onto the hard rock beside her. The waters swirled about his waist as he edged closer. "This is one of the most beautiful places on Earth. It's so private and secluded. Just us within this little slice of paradise."

"Are you always like this with the lasses? Ready to unclothe at a moment's notice?"

"I've never made the Change in front of a woman before. You will be the first. Are you ready?"

She was transfixed, couldn't move her gaze from his heavily muscled chest where a smattering of hair, as dark as his head, trailed down between his contoured abs and disappeared under the water's murky surface. "I'm ready. Shift for me, Finlay. I truly do wish to see your bear."

He took another step closer, his golden eyes heating to a toe-curling hue. "Shifting causes quite a lightning bright display."

"I wield fire. There is naught as bright as that. Shift." The raw intimacy of the moment rolled through her and sparks flared from her fingertips. She sent her fire arcing high into the air then clenched her fists.

"You have such a powerful skill." He eyed the remnants still flickering on her fingertips then he made the Change and bright lights burst in a myriad of sparks. A very large bear with black fur glimmering in the moonlight rose up before her. On his hind legs, he roared.

"Come closer, Finlay." She held out one hand, desperate to touch his beast. "I willnae hurt you."

He slapped his paws down on the boulder either side of her then he nudged her hand with his muzzle.

"Thank you." She took a long breath in, sought the control she needed and sank her fingers into his silky pelt. She scratched between his ears then smiled as a purr rumbled from deep within his chest. The sound caused a strange heat to surge through her, not one of fire, but of something else. A form of heat she'd never experienced before. It pooled between her thighs and made Finlay sniff and prod her belly.

* * * *

Finlay's heartbeat thumped as Arabel petted him, as her fingers slid through his sleek coat and soothed the beast deep within him. Her stunning blue eyes, as warm as a summer sky, held glittering sparks of gold around the edges, and her scent, it swirled so temptingly around him, like honey and something very, very nice. He pushed back a little on his paws and halted. Her shift was wet from the water he'd sprayed as he'd shifted and up this close to her he couldn't help but note the thin ivory cloth pressed against her chest showing the roundness of her full breasts and a tease of pink nipple.

Slowly the fabric dried, likely from her heat and he whimpered. What was she doing to him? She'd invoked so many new emotions from him since he'd entered this secluded area and walked toward her. He should be at the castle as she'd said and searching for his mate, but the deep pull to remain with her had been unbreakable. For five years he'd been searching for his mate in the future, and never had he found her, not even during his search at the village these past few days.

She stroked him, her fingers moving in a delicious massage around his ears and under his chin. He stretched and rubbed against her for more. "Your bear is stunning, Finlay," she murmured in his ear.

He needed more of her touch, of hearing her sweet voice as she spoke so softly and sensuously to him. He prodded her belly again for more.

"I see you like being petted."

A throaty rumble. Her gentle petting soothed him, the first time another's touch had ever done so. He lifted his body higher and she rocked back then wound her arms around his neck to keep from toppling off. He licked her ear and she giggled.

"I cannae believe how soft your pelt is. It feels like furry silk, all smooth and warm. You also feel incredibly big and strong." She touched the tip of her nose to his and smiled, so beautifully his heart missed a beat. "There is something so very intriguing about you."

She more than intrigued him, her long golden locks tumbling to her waist in charming disarray and the moon's glow highlighting her high cheeks and luscious berry-red lips.

"Can you hear me at all, Finlay?"

Her question made him itch to return to her and he forced the Change, so swiftly she gasped. As a man once again, he looked deep into her eyes and said, "I heard every word you uttered, my sweet."

"There isnae a chance I'm *your sweet*." She stroked one finger along his lower lip, her mouth lifting in a teasing smile. "'Tis a shame you're back. I was rather enjoying my chat with your bear."

"My bear adored your touch, as do I."

"You are definitely flirting with me." She picked up his wet shirt lying next to her and passed it to him. "'Tis best you change."

He donned his shirt then planted his hands on the rock either side of her to keep her caged close. "I've never flirted, or shifted in front of a woman before. That is the truth."

"What are you trying to say?" She fixed his collar then lowered her hands.

"Perhaps I should show you." His touched her lower lip just as she'd touched his. "I wish to kiss you, to see if there is something more between us."

"Kissing a fire-wielder isnae permitted. I'm sorry, but I've clearly misled you somehow. You search for your mate and she cannae be me." She scrambled to her feet and jumped from boulder to boulder toward the bank.

"Why is kissing not permitted?" He bounded through the water, hoisted himself onto the boulder in front of her and blocked her way. "Take my hand. These rocks are slippery and I won't have you fall and hurt yourself."

"Kissing isnae permitted because I would lose control of my skill, and in the worst possible way." She shooed him to move.

"I don't think so." He scooped her into his arms then dipped his head and rubbed his cheek against hers. He coated her in his scent, until it clung to her skin and hers clung to him. Aye, his bear demanded this nearness and that he not let her go. He jumped onto the next boulder. "Since my search for my mate began, I've been led in so many different directions, although whenever I've arrived at the place where my mate should be, there was never anyone about, except for the night of the last full moon. For the first time, I was actually driven toward this area."

"Then you received a clear signal she was here." She grasped his shirtfront.

"Aye, and now I have the good fortune of holding you in my arms, I'm aware my mate is close, very close, that she might very well be you."

"That is impossible." She wriggled out of his arms and

jumped onto the mossy bank.

"One can't argue with the mated bond, Arabel, not when it speaks to the very heart of the two who are soul bound." He stepped down beside her. "Do you feel anything toward me?"

"Nay, no' a thing." She frowned something fierce as she eyed his wet shirt. "Allow me to dry you." She smoothed her heated palms over his shoulders and along his chest then circling him, swished along his waist and legs. "That is better. I wouldnae want you to catch a chill."

"All I feel right now is a deep desire to jump back into that loch so when I hop back out, you'll dry me all over again." That need roared to life within him. No woman had ever laid her hands on him the way she just had, the way he wished for her to do again. Her heated touch had been sheer perfection, soft and tender, not harming in the least.

"You fascinate me, Arabel." Gently, he traced the delicate smattering of freckles across her nose and cheeks. "Do I fascinate you at all?"

"I—I—" Confusion crossed her face. "We need to leave." She hurried around the pool toward their clothes, snatched her burgundy gown from the ground and wriggled the velvet over her head. He followed, dressed and fastened his sword and daggers as she fumbled to gather the burgundy ribbons at her back.

"Here, allow me." He slid her long golden locks over one shoulder and exposed the long length of her neck then picked up her gown's ribbons and laced her stays. Gently, he turned her by the shoulders to face him and stroked down her arms to her wrists where her gown's lacy sleeves dangled over the backs of her hands.

"Oh, your hair is still wet. We cannae have that." She ran her fingers through his shoulder-length hair, drying and tidying it, the delicious contact sending a wave of warmth across his scalp. "Is that better?"

"Infinitely. I love having your hands on me."

"You must cease talking like that." She swayed toward him and the golden sparks rimming her blue eyes glimmered before she jolted upright. "'Tis time to leave."

"Not without me." He collected his horse. "I'm your guard."

"I've roamed these forest paths my entire life. I assure you I dinnae need a guard." She walked toward the trail, the sensual sway of her hips making him want to drag her into his arms and hold her close, to smother her with even more of his scent. The desire roared through him, demanding and relentless, a need that wouldn't be appeased. His bear had found his mate and so had he, only it appeared now he'd need to convince her of that fact.

Within minutes they emerged from the woods and the thick stone walls of the House of Clan Matheson rose like an impenetrable fortress in the dark. A two-story gatehouse took pride of place in front while beyond the gate's arch, the four-story north tower house overlooked all. He stopped at the stables and handed his steed to the stable hand who hurried over to him then slung his traveling bag over one shoulder and guided Arabel through the gates and across the inner courtyard. So few of her clansmen would likely be awake at this late hour of the night, other than the guards, but since he didn't wish to wander through the great hall and disturb those warriors who had already sought their rest, he led her toward the side stairs. "Where is your chamber?"

"On the third floor." She climbed the stairs and walked along the gloomy corridor lit only by the odd candle in an iron wall sconce. The passageway remained bare of any other, each of the doors leading from it firmly shut, except for the last one. She walked inside the chamber that remained perfectly dark with not even the fire lit.

"Is this your room alone?" He followed her inside.

"It is. Which of the guest chambers have you been given?"

"On the night I arrived, I bedded down on a pallet in the great hall alongside the other warriors. I needed to remain close to the door in case my bear wished to roam, which he did in no time at all. He's been antsy this past week." But not anymore. His bear had settled with one gentle petting from her. The only woman who would be able to do that would be his mate. He set his bag down near the side table and faced her. "We were provided with all we'd need and since I've arrived, I've traveled light, as have my brothers and Isla."

"If you wish, I can ask one of the maids to prepare a chamber for you." She brought fire forth to one fingertip and lit a candle in the corner stand. Its glow flickered over her queen-sized bed with its red velvet canopy sweeping down onto the polished wooden floors.

"There's no need." He intended to stay right here where he could be close to her. "Would you like your fire lit and your chamber warmed?"

"I can manage to light my own fire. Fire-wielder, remember?" Grinning, she crossed to the window where a chilly breeze fluttered through and closed it. "I truly am fine now, my skill back under control. You can leave and be assured I'm well."

"I can't leave you, not right now." He stepped up to her, rested his hands on her shoulders and breathed in her delectable warm scent. A gentle peace invaded his soul. Holding her soothed him. He wouldn't forget this moment, the one in which he'd most certainly found his mate. Over her head out the window, the white-capped waves rolled into shore and across the bay, a sail shimmered in the moonlight then disappeared into the dark farther along the inland channel toward MacKenzie land. He'd also found her before the coming battle. Relief rolled through him. "This feels so good, standing here with you."

"I'm glad you and your brothers are here to aid us in saving the village." She slid one hand over his, her touch so soft, so gentle. His bear purred deep inside him and demanded a closer touch.

"Aye, and we won't leave until we have."

"The village is so exposed on the tip and we'll have so very little warning when the MacKenzie attacks. It does no' help that this is a busy waterway and intersects with Loch Carron and Loch Hourn."

"We can still guard these waterways well from this prominent location." He slipped one arm around her waist and drew her closer still, a hold she didn't pull away from. His bear settled even further.

"A location the MacKenzie too desires, one he intends to take, although I too will never allow him to harm the villagers. He took my parents' lives but he won't take another of my kin. I swear it, on my life."

"The MacKenzie killed your parents?" He frowned and searched her gaze. Such deep loss swirled within her beautiful eyes and that emotion bubbled up and rose within him as well. "Tell me how it happened."

"No' long after Julia and I came of age, Father entered into negotiations for Julia's marriage to the Chief of MacKenzie's third son. At the time we were allies, no' yet at war as we currently are. The MacKenzie requested a meeting, but 'twas just a ruse. As soon as my parents arrived at his castle, he had them tossed into the dungeon and then sent a demand to Gilleoin. My uncle was told to hand over his lands on the tip of Loch Alsh and in return the MacKenzie would release our parents. For several months demands volleyed back and forth until Gilleoin realized the MacKenzie would never listen to reason. That's when he set out for their stronghold with an elite contingency of his warriors. His intention was to sneak in under the cover of darkness, rescue my parents and then return with them. Instead Gilleoin discovered my parents had been slain at the MacKenzie's own hand, several months prior, afore the first demand had even been sent. He is a snake."

"What did Gilleoin do?" Rage simmered and he barely held it down. The MacKenzie had hurt his woman, something he'd never allow again.

"Gilleoin was furious and he attacked with great force then left a bloody trail in his wake. Now the MacKenzie is determined to have his retribution, to ensure he takes all Gilleoin holds as precious. Those of fae blood mingle strongly with Gilleoin's firstborn line and the MacKenzie fears the strength we'll gain from being aligned." Heat flared from her, flapped his hair about his shoulders and rippled the thick red bed canopy behind him. She gasped and jerked away. "I'm sorry. Did I hurt you?"

"Not at all. I can handle your small flares, likely better than anyone else can." He wrapped his arms around her, tucked her cheek against his chest and savored her closeness. Aye, his feelings for her were strong. Never had another woman ever brought such tender emotions to roaring life within him. From this moment forth, he wouldn't be leaving her side, not until she'd accepted their bond and the fact that they were mated.

"You would never be able to handle a strong flare, and I cannae lose any more of my fae kin, Finlay."

"You won't, not now my brothers and I are here." He stroked her back until she snuggled closer. "Do you feel better?"

"A little, but I shouldn't allow this kind of touch. I'm no' quite sure why I have."

"Because we are one and the same."

"We're not mated."

"Then try and pull away."

She pressed her hands to his chest as if she would, only she sighed and dropped them again. "An anomaly for sure. I've changed my mind. Could you please light my fire?"

"Of course." He released her even though he didn't wish to and crouched before the hearth. From a log set in a basket at the side, he tore strips off it then brought a flame to life striking flint with his dagger. Once the fire roared and spread its heat throughout the room, he rose and dusted his hands. "Would you like me to unlace your gown so you can ready yourself for bed?"

"If you dinnae mind." She turned her back and held her

burgundy bodice to her chest.

"I'll never mind." He sank his fingers into her long golden-blond locks, the soft strands sliding like silk across his wrists and forearms. He eased her hair over her shoulder and exposed her back. "You have the most glorious hair. It glows like woven silk in the firelight."

"It does?" Over her shoulder, she frowned.

"Aye, and your eyes—" They sparkled like sapphires, a most striking hue with that glittering flare of gold at the edge. "I could drown in them."

"Mayhap I shouldnae have invited you into my chamber." She raised a brow. "Doing so has clearly given you the wrong idea."

"You didn't invite me. I entered of my own free will, and I would do so again and again." He loosened her lacings and unable to help himself with the sight of her neck on magnificent display again, he brushed a kiss against the long column, wishing he could damn well take a bite instead. They'd be time for that later, once he'd assured her of the depth of their bond and his commitment to her. "In the future, women rarely need aid in dressing themselves."

"How is that?"

"There are many new inventions, like zips. They have sharp metal teeth that slide together when pulled shut. I don't know quite how you deal with all these layers of fabric."

"As a child, I used to sneak a pair of trews from one of the lads when I wished to roam the woods with complete freedom. Sometimes I still do." With her bodice scrunched in her hands, she toed off her silk slippers then foraged for her nightgown in the trunk under the window before stepping behind a silk dressing screen hand-painted with a stunning field of heather.

"It's dangerous for you to roam the woods on your own." He paced her chamber, unease tracking through him. Brigands would lie in wait for just such a tempting morsel as his woman.

"Dinnae forget my skill, Finlay. One such as I hardly needs

a guard. I hold one of deadliest of the fae battle skills. 'Tis just a shame I am a woman and no one allows me to use it." Her gown flopped over the top of the screen then she rustled about.

He itched to slip behind that screen and tell her exactly why she did need a guard, that it would be him and only him in the future. Instead he bunched his fists and remained right where he was. "Do you dress for bed often with male company in your room?"

"Never." She walked out, all her luscious curves hidden from his sight in a white nightgown, or at least she was hidden until she stepped between him and the golden glow of the fire. The flames lit the outline of her shapely legs to sheer perfection.

"You are a sight to behold." Touch was vitally important to any shifter, and more so between mates. He closed the distance between them and caught her hands. "Arabel, from the moment I met you, I've been drawn to you, and right now I couldn't leave you if I tried. These new emotions flaring to life within in me would only rise when I'm with my chosen one. I need you to believe that."

"I'm no' your chosen one." She stepped away and the distance she enforced had his bear rumbling his displeasure. "You must keep searching, Finlay, and I shall aid you on the morrow if you wish. I know all the lasses."

"My bear wants you, and only you." His claws sliced out. "He's hungry for his mate, and there is no arguing with either him or me." She was his, and of that he had no doubt. A fire-wielder. Aye, her skill would provide a greater challenge than most mated pairs had to deal with, but it was a challenge he was more than up for. They were soul-bound, a match in every way, and he wouldn't allow her skill to obstruct his path, of completing the bond and ensuring she never left his side.

Chapter 2

Standing on the pebbly beach before the fae village, Nessa wrapped her fur cloak tighter about her as moonlight shimmered across the loch's choppy surface. Farther along the bay, the House of Clan Matheson rose like a sentinel in the dark, its massive gray stone turrets and towering walls topped with battlements and guardsmen roaming the ramparts. From the multitude of square windows, candlelight flickered in welcome. Her sanctuary, and that of her fae people, if only they'd accept it.

The village leaders had heeded her first forewarning and spoken to the people, but as she'd had no further visions surrounding the battle since then, they now believed all would be well and that they could adequately defend their village and their people. That would not be the case. If only she could force a vision.

"Mother!" Sorcha hurried through the gate in the high stone wall surrounding the village, her hands clasped in her thick blue woolen skirts. Behind her, the houses of stone and clay, cloistered so tightly together, would soon be naught but dust if she couldn't convince all within to defy the leaders and seek the safety that awaited them within Gilleoin's walls.

Sorcha joined her on the beach, a little breathless. "What are you doing out here in the cold?"

"Julia is on her way." A vision had shown her Arabel's latest flare and their conversation about the four elements.

"'Tis late. Why does she come?" Sorcha wrapped her plaid tighter about her shoulders.

"She worries for Arabel and with very good reason. There is now cold-fire present within her aura."

"Oh dear." Sorcha clasped a hand to her mouth and glanced out at sea.

A skiff came into view with Julia seated at the bow, her golden locks whipping about her in the brisk breeze and the boat's white sail pulled taut.

It cruised across the sea, and as a large wave rolled in, the warrior in command of it lowered the sail, gripped the boat's rudder and skimmed toward the land. As he neared, he jumped into the waist-deep water, seized the bow and hauled the skiff in between two half-beached birlinns. With his white tunic fluttering over his black trews, the warrior swung her granddaughter onto the beach.

Julia hurried toward her, her forest-green skirts bunched in her white-knuckled hands.

"I'm here, my dear." Nessa opened her arms and Julia ran into them.

"Arabel's cold-fire rises, Grandmother. I'm so worried."

"Aye, I saw all that happened at the pool as well as your conversation. 'Tis well and truly possible that the newcomers' arrival has upset the balance of the elements. I wouldnae be surprised if that is the case at all."

"Then how do we fix the imbalance?"

"Through a realignment. Fire, water, air and earth must once again join together as one and until that happens, something only nature can provide, you must keep your sister close. Her cold-fire could easily rise again and she will need all of us in the coming days, more so than ever afore."

"Aye. I'll remain close by her side. That I promise you."

"Good." And she'd continue to remain alert until the realignment occurred. Arabel's life was at stake, as well as her people's lives here at the village. There was nothing she wouldn't do, not for any of them.

Chapter 3

"You and your bear are clearly confused. We arena mated." Arabel opened her chamber door and motioned for Finlay to leave. She couldn't be his chosen one, no matter the soul deep ache in her chest had finally eased for the first time in days.

"I'm not leaving you, Arabel. Doing so is no longer possible, and I don't mean to be difficult, I'm just stating the facts." He removed his belted sword and daggers, placed them on top of the side table and bolted her door.

"I didnae say you could stay." Yet deep inside, a part of her rejoiced he was. Goodness. What had the man done to her? Her thoughts were completely out of order, which was so unlike her.

"It's late and I'm tired. I'll take the chair for the night. May I borrow a pillow?"

"You cannae sleep in my chamber, no matter what you believe."

"No one will know I've remained, apart from you and me." He strode to her bed, snatched one of the pillows then dropped into the corner navy padded chair. Pillow plumped, he tucked it behind his head then leaned back and crossed his booted feet at the ankle, his gaze on hers. "Seek your sleep, my mate. I'll not disturb you."

"Now you think to call me your mate?"

"Because you are."

"Are you always this annoying?" Arms crossed, she tapped one foot, her nightrail swishing about her ankles.

"Only around those who are the most important to me, and right now you are at the very top of that list." He motioned toward the candle in the corner stand. "Don't forget to blow that out before you close your eyes."

"I'm a fire-wielder. Being mated to me would ensure your death, and no' just a pleasant one either. There would be a raging fire and scorching involved."

"Then hopefully we'll both learn how to keep your fire under control."

"When a fire-wielder lies with a man, he dies." She tapped her other foot. "My skill is one of the rarest amongst the villagers, and the six fire-wielders who've come afore me have all passed, right after they wed and allowed an intimacy their skill forbid them. In the moment when they'd joined with their loved one, they killed them with their loss of control. Then in their grief, they allowed their cold-fire to consume them, to ice their blood and cease their heart from beating. After the passing of the last fire-wielder, the village leaders decreed that none with my skill could ever be allowed such an intimacy again, a decree I will gladly uphold."

"We'll find a way to get around your skill." He arched a brow, rather challengingly. "We're soul bound, which means there is nothing we can't overcome if we truly wish to be together." He stood and pointed at the bed. "Get in there now, or else I'll put you in there, and join you."

"You clearly didnae listen to a word I just said. You are so frustrating." She huffed, blew out the candle and clambered in underneath her fur bedcovers while Finlay strode to her hearth and stared at the flames. The fire's glow flickered across his high cheeks and lit the shoulder-length ends of his midnight-black hair, turning it a glorious sizzling blue. He was one of the most striking men she'd ever beheld, and it certainly didn't help that everything about him called to her, from his current fiery mood to the teasingly sensuous smile that had lifted his lips earlier at the loch. Aye, she was entranced by him, just as she shouldn't be. "I cannae sleep if you're going to stare at the fire all night, Finlay."

"I've spoken the truth about the two of us being mated. I know the difference between how I've felt being around you and every other lass I've ever known."

"There's no full moon." That was the only night when their senses could truly lead them to their chosen ones. "So you must be mistaken."

"There's no mistake. I've been searching for you for five long years, which includes dozens of full moons, and I know you are mine." He gazed at her bed, his fingers twitching at his sides. "I'm itching to join you, to hold you through the night. Already I can't stand this distance and it's only a few feet."

His words sent a shimmer of heat through her. Good grief, how annoying. "You can stay right where you are."

"Or I could join you. I give you my word I'll do no more than hold you through the night. It would ease both our frustration." He kicked off his boots and sauntered closer, his move so like that of a bear on the prowl for a tasty treat. She should tell him to return to the chair, only the words wouldn't move past her lips. Instead, she watched wide-eyed as he rolled in under the covers and faced her. "May I touch you, Arabel?"

"You clearly have a death wish."

"No, my only wish has ever been to find my chosen one and never let her go." He stroked one hand over her hip, drew her a touch closer, until the blazing heat of his body stamped itself right into her.

"I—" She couldn't turn away from his desire-filled eyes, didn't even have a chance to. "Tell me more about you and your kin, Finlay."

"What would you like to know?"

"Whatever you wish to share."

"My parents are mated and my father is the chief of our clan. Of my two brothers, Iain is the eldest by a couple of minutes, and Kirk younger than me by the same length of time. We also share a brotherly bond that allows us to sense each other's emotions."

"You do?" How incredible. "Can you sense their emotions now?"

"Iain's are the strongest, the most ecstatic, and I'd say he's abed with Isla."

"Oh dear, you can tell when he's—" She pressed a hand to her mouth, her cheeks flushing with heat. "What of Kirk?"

"Kirk's curiosity is strong. He can sense my sudden contentment since it's no doubt blasting down our line." He swept her golden hair back and exposed her neck. "I'm also the most competitive of the three of us, as well as the most level-headed."

"You are hardly level-headed, no' when you wish to tangle with me."

A low growl rumbled from his throat and his claws sliced out.

"Your bear doesn't approve of my estimation?" She fluffed her pillow and tucked it more securely under her head.

"Ignore my bear."

"Your bear is impossible to ignore. He's both sizeable and pushy, as is the man."

"I haven't even begun to get pushy with you yet." He leaned closer, claws retracting as he touched his nose to hers. "But when I do, you'll know, because I intend to enjoy a bite or two of you."

Gilleoin was always biting Aunt Sorcha, and now Kenneth, her cousin and Gilleoin's firstborn son, had mated with Elizabeth, a good friend of hers from the village and since that day, her friend too had sported red marks on her neck. Love bites, Elizabeth had called them.

"Have you ever bitten a lass afore?" she asked him.

"When a shifter bites his mate and his mate bites him, it is a mark of claim. It's also an aphrodisiac to both the giver and the receiver." His hungry gaze slid to her neck. "The need to bite you is strong."

"An aphro-dis-iac?" She stumbled over the unknown word. "What exactly do you mean?"

"Our bite excites sexual desire, which means we only ever bite our chosen ones."

She smoothed her palm over her neck and her now throbbing pulse. Warmth rippled out from the spot and made her heat in places she had no wish to heat. "Biting sounds barbaric."

"Would you like to see if it is?" Another glimmer of challenge lit his eyes.

"You are a terrible tease."

"As are you." He curled his hand more firmly around her hip and sighed in complete contentment. "Thank you for allowing me in your bed."

"I hardly had a choice."

"And that likely won't change."

Goodness. How was she to argue with him when he was like this?

Instead, she closed her eyes and breathed out, silently seeking a much needed reprieve.

"Rest well, my sweet." His possessive hold tightened. "I shall be here when you awaken."

Since she couldn't argue with him, she allowed the dark to envelope her and slowly flittered toward sleep, his hold so heavenly warm. How frustrating.

* * * *

The early morning sunshine beamed through Arabel's narrow window and stirred her from her slumber far sooner than she wished. She stretched and burrowed her nose deeper into the covers, which had suddenly become more like firm flesh with a delicious pine and fresh water scent. She lifted one eyelid and gasped.

Her legs were tangled with Finlay's and she lay half over top of him. She should move away, only her heat hadn't arisen at this very intimate contact when it should have. Unable to help herself, she spread her hand fully over his solid chest and reveled as his muscles flexed under her touch. He looked so rumpled and delicious with a razz of stubble on his jaw and his black hair catching the morning light and gleaming like silk. "Finlay?" she whispered.

No answer. He slept soundly, his tunic gaping at the top and half off his shoulder. A stunning Celtic mark etched upon his bicep peeked out.

She slid her hand under the fabric and eased his sleeve farther down his arm. With one finger, she gently traced over the woven mark. So beautiful. Oh, and so was all the golden skin she'd exposed. She caressed his flesh, her heartbeat pounding as she did. 'Twas wonderful to touch him so freely. She leaned in, pressed her lips against the woven mark then nibbled up and over his shoulder toward the delectable looking hollow where his shoulder met his neck. Mmm, he tasted delicious too, an intoxicating mix of hard man and smooth skin. She razzed her teeth back and forth over his flesh then sucked his skin between her lips.

"Arabel?" He spoke her name, so softly, so sensually. "Hell, I love the feel of your mouth on me. Do it."

"Do what?" she murmured.

"I want your mark." His long black lashes swept up and his golden gaze met hers, so smolderingly hot. Then slowly, succinctly, he palmed the back of her head and brought her mouth back to his neck. "Bite me, my sweet. There is nothing you need to be afraid of."

"I wasnae about to bite you." Drat it. There she went again nibbling on his flesh. She needed to pull away, only everything within her cried out at the thought of stopping.

"Harder," he pushed. "Don't deny me what I want."

Beyond frustrated, she bit him, just as he'd asked and the moment she released his skin, he flipped her over onto her back, buried his head at her neck and pressed his entire body against hers. Every inch of him was aligned with every inch of her and his manhood, so very hard and hot, dug into her belly. "You make me lose my mind," she gasped. "We must cease this nonsense."

"There is no stopping the mated bond when it takes form." He licked her skin, right over her pounding pulse. "My bear is raging at me, demanding I take you and make you ours."

"Wait." She gripped his shoulders, fingernails digging into his flesh. She wanted to push him away, but she couldn't, actually whimpered when she tried to. "Demanding this bond will ensure your death, Finlay, and I will never take the life of another, especially yours."

"You've given me a reason to live, not taken my life away." He tipped her head back farther, exposed her entire neck and scraped his teeth back and forth over her flesh. "Say aye. I need to mark you as you just marked me, but I need your permission first."

"'Tis sheer luck my fire has no' yet flared. Usually I cannae handle this much touch with another." She shuddered in his arms and heat rippled through her and pooled between her thighs, the wrong kind of heat.

He breathed deep with one sensual grin. "Mmm, you smell like honey, one of my favorite treats. It's like liquid gold to my bear and I could eat it by the tubful, just as I could eat you."

"I want to say aye, but there is too much danger in doing so." She couldn't deny the need that had rolled through her to mark him, and the sheer pleasure that had taken hold once she had.

"Those who are soul bound to one another can't harm each other. I can guarantee you your fire will never singe a hair on my head, ever. It's impossible." He licked down her neck to the top rise of her breasts and her nipples beaded into hard, pulsing points. "There has also never been another woman I have ever touched as I've touched you, and even without the aid of the current full moon, everything within me screams that you're my mated one."

His words touched her heart and his heavenly hold made her crave more. "Touch me, but be careful."

"I'll take the utmost care." He cupped her breasts through her thin cotton shift, lifted them higher until the upper swells were fully exposed then swept his tongue across each rise.

Sweet heaven. His touch was glorious and made her want so much more. She arched into him and heat sizzled under her skin in a swift flare she couldn't contain. Nay. She wouldn't burn him. She shoved him back, rolled free and scrambled out of the bed. A bolt of pain speared through her. Moving away from him hurt, as if her very soul had been wrenched away from his. "I'm sorry, Finlay."

"No, this is my fault. Clearly I didn't take enough care." He was out of the bed in an instant and crouching in front of her, his thumb moving in a slow circle over the mark she'd given him.

* * * *

Finlay mentally berated himself. The thought of hurting Arabel in any way pained him.

"Is there still heat coming from me?" She shoved up a hand. "And stay right where you are while you check."

"There is heat but you haven't burnt me, and you won't." The last thing he wanted to do was make her feel uneasy, not when she was his to care for. "You are the first fire-wielder to mate with a shifter and I agree that makes things difficult, but perhaps we've been bound together for a greater purpose. Certainly I can handle a higher degree of your heat as none other can."

"You cannae handle a full blast. Please, step aside." He moved and she nodded her thanks. "Where there's heat, there is fire." She dunked her hands into the pitcher of cold water on the side table and steam plumed. "See, heat. Fire is just a blink or two away."

"And when there's a mated bond, there are two souls entwined and two people who can't live without each other. You are the only woman I will ever live for, the only one who'll make my life complete."

"I—" She gaped at his bare legs. "When did you take your kilt off?"

"During the night. I got hot, and my shirt covers me adequately, not that I have any issue with being unclothed before you. I was nude in the pool last night."

"The waters were dark and you well know that." She tossed him his bag from under the table. "Please, don some clothing."

"As you wish." Whatever would make her feel more ease, he'd do. He flipped the flap open and removed a pair of black leather pants and a tan colored shirt. He changed, rolled the billowy sleeves of the shirt to his elbow and donned his pants. "Is this better, my mate?"

"Nay—I mean aye. Much better." She set her hands on her hips. "We need to have a talk, a serious one."

"We do." He caught one of her long golden-blond locks, wound the length around his finger then released it. It bounced and caught the tip of her cute nose. Everything about her intrigued him.

"Finlay!" She flicked the lock away. "Cease playing with my hair. I need you to understand just how much danger you're in when you insist on touching me."

"I apologize, but the need to touch you rages through me." He backed her against the wall, slid one hand behind her head and the other behind her shoulders so she'd not scrape her flesh on the rough stone. Then slowly, he bent his head. "May I kiss you?" He longed to taste her lips. "One single kiss. I need this, Arabel. I need you."

"There shall be no kissing."

"Then I shall just have to steal a kiss."

"There shall be no stealing of kisses either." She ducked under his arm, gone in the blink of an eye as she darted to her golden curtained ambry across the room. She nabbed a blue and gold colored gown and disappeared behind her dressing screen. "Perhaps you should leave."

"And go where?"

"Anywhere but near me."

"That is an impossible request."

"I also have much to do this day, my sister to find and further preparations to make for any of the villagers who I hope will be seeking shelter from the coming battle behind these walls. I'm sure you have plenty to do to keep you occupied too. There is a village to save, and all." Velvet swished.

"So you intend to ignore the fact we're mated and a bond has formed?" Something he wouldn't allow. Boots in hand, he pulled them on then strapped his wrist daggers and sword belt in place. From the side table, he picked up the pitcher of water and poured some into the basin. Steam curled into the air. Nice. "Thank you, my sweet, for heating the water."

"You are completely impossible," she grumbled from behind the screen. "I didnae heat it for you."

"Aye, but I still appreciate it all the same." He chuckled. His woman had a fiery temper, one that made him gloriously happy. He'd always hoped his woman would be as feisty and strong-willed as he was, and she was no disappointment. With the bar of soap in hand, he built up a good lather and before the looking glass propped on the table, smeared the suds over his jaw. Dagger unsheathed, he gently ran the blade in one slow stroke from his ear to his chin, thankfully only nicking his skin the once. He sure missed the modern conveniences of his own time.

Arabel strode out, a radiant vision in long layers of blue that matched her eyes to perfection. Even the gold lace at her wrists and along the hem of her full skirts matched the flecks in her eyes. Such a sight to behold. "You look beautiful."

"Please watch what you're doing. If you slice your throat and bleed all over my floor, I willnae be happy." She stepped in behind him, lifted his shoulder-length hair, her gaze meeting his in the glass. "What are your intentions for this day?"

"To find my brothers and Isla. I need to speak to Isla about those who've held your skill over the centuries. She's from Kenneth's line and her clan live right here in the future. There is also little that passes her by. If there's a way to get around this intimacy issue of yours, I need to find it, and right now she's my best option." He pulled his collar to the side and exposed the mark she'd given him. "I will of course inform them all I've found my chosen one."

"Careful with that blade. You're waving it all over the place. Allow me." She turned him by the shoulders to face her, pressed him down until his backside rested on the table then held out her hand for his dagger. "I'll shave you, otherwise we shall be here all day."

"I'd love to be here all day."

"I'm sure you would. Dagger, now."

"Aye, but take care. You seem to be in a fierce mood, one I've put you in, but still..." He passed her his blade, cupped her hips and held her steady between his spread legs. "Do you shave men often?"

"On occasion, if a warrior has been injured and requires aid." Turning his cheek with one finger, she held the blade nice and close to his skin and ran it in a smooth line down. Carefully, she drew the dagger along the next portion under his chin and down his throat. "Tell me more about the future, and why you are so terrible at shaving yourself."

"In the future, we have electric shavers. They are a device which plugs into a power source called electricity and when the shaver is turned on, the device has sharp metal rotating heads that slice the stubble off at the root. No soap and blade is necessary."

"Oh, I see. And what is this elec-tri-city?" She twisted her tongue around the foreign word. "Is that correct?"

"Aye, and electricity is energy that's been harnessed and contained. That's done in various ways and then when the electricity is needed, the energy is dispersed and can do a multitude of things. Like bringing heat and light into a room, powering devices big and small, allowing communication between people all over the world, that sort of thing.

"That sounds farfetched. Surely people cannae speak to each other all over the world, and please, dinnae move. Each time you do you run the risk of being cut." She ran the blade right under his nose. "I wouldnae wish to nick this beautiful mouth of yours."

"You find my mouth—"

"Dinnae speak either." She tapped his jaw shut and giggled. The sound of her laughter lightened his heart. Hell, he adored seeing her smile. She continued to shave him, around his lips then along the last stretch of his neck and after she was done, she dabbed his skin dry with the cloth. "Take a look in the glass. What do you think?"

Observing his reflection, he patted his jawline and traced around his lips. "You've done a better job than I ever could have."

"Wonderful." She picked up the fine bone comb on the table, brushed his hair until the dark strands curled around her fingers then nodded. "All done."

"My thanks." He wiped his blade clean, sheathed it at his wrist then tucked his traveling bag out of the way next to her trunk under the window.

Before the glass, she combed her hair and secured her pale locks at each side with a silver pin. Done, she set it down and faced him. "Are you ready to break your fast, Finlay?"

"Always. I'm hungry this morning, and for far more than breakfast." He caught her around the waist and drew her closer. "I have a proposition."

"That sounds dangerous." She seized his biceps and held on. "We really need to cease touching."

"Allow me one kiss before we leave. I've yet to taste your lips and I fear I'll be overcome with the desire to do so and at the worst possible time." He was quite serious. "I've been searching for you for the longest time and I can't seem to hold back any of my desires, which are growing rapidly the more time we spend together. It's also best we test your limits well away from your kin."

"That is a terrible proposition." Yet a glimmer of hope flared in her eyes. She wanted his kiss, and with a little nudge, he might be able to claim one from her.

"We'll take things slowly. I promise you I will. This time I'll be far more careful." He caressed her sides, roamed down and scooped her bottom. Lifted higher, he pressed his hips against hers. "Say, aye."

"You are one very pushy bear."

"Is that an aye?"

"One kiss, then you shall see we are a terrible match and hopefully head straight for the hills."

"Perfect." He'd take her agreement for a kiss no matter how it was offered. Gently, he carried her to the bed and laid her across the soft brown fur bedcovering then nudged her knees apart and with his legs between hers, sank down on top of her. "I will never desire any other than you."

"Must we lie down for this kiss?" She wriggled underneath him, her breath catching.

"Aye, that would be my preference."

"I feel too hot." She closed her eyes. "And there are butterflies taking flight in my belly. Can we hurry and be done with this?"

"We can, the moment you look at me."

She opened her eyes and frowned. "You are completely relentless."

"Because losing you is something I'll never survive, not now that I've finally found you." He lowered his head a touch and completed the trap. "After this kiss, I want the right to sleep in your bed, each and every night."

"You are beyond relentless."

"If you need me to taper my needs back, just ask."

"As if you'd listen." She rolled her eyes and he chuckled.

"You are already coming to know me so well." Slowly he brushed his mouth over hers, her lips so achingly soft as he joined them together. Playfully, he nipped her lower lip, sucked it into his mouth then licked her tongue. Desire swarmed his senses and as her breasts swelled under his chest, a raw and primal sensation speared through him. He rubbed his body against hers, until his scent surrounded her and hers enveloped him.

"I cannae believe we're kissing." Her breath whispered softly across his lips in a teasing caress he hungered for more of. "A little more, Finlay, please."

She nibbled on his lips and he groaned, deep and throaty before capturing her mouth and offering her the kiss she'd asked for. An intense need he couldn't resist flooded him.

"Arabel, I love how you feel underneath me, all soft curves and glorious heat." With painstaking slowness, he grazed a finger along the upper swell of her breasts where her heart-shaped neckline dipped.

"I shouldnae be allowing this." She squeezed her eyes shut and when she opened them again, she gazed into his eyes. "One more kiss since I have no' burnt you just yet."

"Do you feel the depth of need our bond demands?"

"Aye, and 'tis most frustrating." She kissed him, a deep and devouring kiss that made his heartbeat pound and hers flutter into a frenzy against his. "This is bad, very bad." She nipped his earlobe before trailing her lips down his neck to the very spot where she'd bitten him earlier. She laved the mark she'd made and he bent his head to her neck, trapping and keeping her locked in place.

"I give you my oath, Arabel. You will always have my protection, my absolute devotion and undying loyalty. Whatever you need, I intend to provide."

"I feel—I feel too much." She scrapped her teeth back and

forth over his skin. "I should be able to deny what's happening. Your very life is at stake if I dinnae."

"You're my mate and we are soul bound. What you desire is what I desire, and that is the completion of our bond." He lifted one arm and his skin rippled with the Change. Soft fur, the same color as the hair on his head, shimmered then retracted. "My bear rides me hard. He knows you're ours."

"When did you first know, that your mate wouldn't be easy to find?"

"Very young, maybe six or seven. There were no female cubs of a similar age to me within my clan." He slid her hair back from her shoulder and eased the sleeve of her gown to the side.

"Are you going to bite me?"

"Aye, if you'll permit it. Until you're ready to complete the bond and join fully as one, we both need this, to hold each other's mark."

"You won't push for that completion?" Her first words of true acceptance, and the sheer beauty of them sang to his soul.

"Not when I wish for you to come to me of your own free will, although I do fully intend to entice you, as much as is humanly possible." Head lowered, his breath fanned her skin then he closed his eyes, his bear prowling under his skin. "Do you agree, Arabel? May I bite you?"

Chapter 4

Within the village along the loch, Isla Matheson awoke with Iain wrapped around her. Her shifter mate had become extremely overprotective since they'd arrived in this time and Nessa had informed her of the babies she carried. Still, she'd traveled through time just as Iain and his brothers had because she too was needed in this coming war, and as one who held the skill of compelling there was so much she could do to give aid.

"Iain?" She gave him a little shake. "It's morning and I can't move until you do."

"I prefer that you don't move at all. I like this position and having you close."

"I'm sure you do." She slid his rumpled black shoulder-length hair to the side then nuzzled his neck. The mark she'd placed there three days ago had faded and her mouth watered to make a new one, to ensure all who saw him were well aware he was hers. Gently, she razzed her teeth over his most sensitive spot and sucked his skin into her mouth.

He groaned, one heavenly deep rumble before he stretched and pressed his thickening shaft into her hip. "My love, this is the very best way to wake me."

"I'm rather partial to it too. Do you mind if I bite you?"

"I'll only mind if you don't."

"Perfect, because I'm very hungry." Unable to wait another moment, she bit down and claimed the man who was hers in every way. He jerked, his breath catching then he bit her in return and lapped her skin until tingles rippled through her body and she desired a whole lot more than his bite alone. Aye, this was the very best way to awaken.

Slow and sensual touches followed, sexy kisses that made her lose her mind, and his carnal gaze on hers as he slid so perfectly inside her. She reveled in the moment, in the sheer perfection of two soul bound mates coming together in such harmony. This bond was what every shifter desired and lived for. It was what she wanted for her kin back home, to have the hope restored to them, that their chosen one would await them as her mate had awaited her. She also desperately desired the same bond for Finlay and Kirk, would do anything to aid them in finding their mates.

Iain lifted up a touch and murmured in her ear, "Are you ready to return to the castle?"

"Aye, Finlay has need of us. Last night before he left, he spoke to me of his certainty that his mate was close."

"Then we'll find Kirk and leave. I long for my brothers to find their chosen ones, just as I have found you." Iain rose from their bed and lifted her to her feet as he did.

The 'power of three' were at their strongest when they stood together. A formidable presence she too stood beside, no matter what trials or tribulations lay ahead. Certainly the battle to come would be one they would all fight. Iain's desires were hers, including all that he was, and she wanted it no other way.

Chapter 5

Arabel wanted Finlay's mark with a deep, burning need, one that hardened her nipples into tight points. "You are beyond enticing, Finlay, and a dream I've never allowed myself to have, being with another."

"Does that mean I can bite you?" He slid his hand inside her bodice and cupped her breast. He thumbed the pebbled peak then dipped his head and licked it. The hot stroke of his tongue sent heat racing to her core and she arched her back and moaned.

"I cannae think straight, and I'm hot, too hot." Her nipple throbbed, all achy and wet from his kiss.

"There is no heat. You're in complete control, whether you feel that way or not."

"You're wrong. I have next to no control when you touch me the way you do."

"Do you wish for me to stop?"

"No biting me yet. Kiss me again."

"I'll take whatever you're prepared to give. Kissing it is." He urged her lips apart and plunged his tongue inside her mouth. His kiss was divine and held an edge of hunger that matched her own. Desire rushed through her and she pressed her breasts against his chest and welcomed every new and needy emotion that raged through her. She stroked down his sides and roamed over his rear. Encased in hip-hugging leather pants, his tight buttocks rocked in her grasp, his shaft full and poking into her belly.

A deep craving for more flooded her and her heat flared, rippled with a wave across the bed curtains and made the wooden posts creak as they expanded. "Finlay, I'm losing control."

"I can sense it. You're far hotter than before." He lifted himself from her, his heavenly weight gone from one breath to the next, then he seized the half-filled pail under the side table and held it over top of her. "Do you wish for this?"

"Aye."

He poured and steam billowed.

Slowly, ever so slowly her body cooled but not the deep and aching desire she had for him. What was she going to do about this desperate need for more that had taken her over? If he ever did mark her, she'd likely burst into flames, and honestly, she could no longer deny how much she wanted him to mark her as she'd marked him. They were mated, and the bond had taken ahold of her with a fierce intensity she couldn't deny. Never had she felt so alive than when she'd been in his arms, and the thought of being without him, it brought pain to her very soul.

"I want you." Tears misted her gaze. "And I hate having to push you away."

"I understand why you must, and all will be well, no matter the challenges that lie ahead of us. Keep the faith that we'll meet them together. Because we will, and always at each other's side." He set the pail down and extended a hand to her. "Have you cooled sufficiently?"

"I have, and I need to remain that way." She slid her fingers around his and he tugged her to her feet, her gown drying with a mere thought as she stood.

"We're soul bound, Arabel, and we'll work around your skill, because I intend to join with you. You will be mine, forever, just as I will be yours."

"Your safety comes first, above all things." She'd never concede on that.

"I agree, just as your safety too comes first." He slid one finger under her chin, kept her gaze firmly on his. "Glad I am that you've finally accepted all that we will be."

"I will never burn you." She stood by that conviction. She'd gladly take her own life before she ever harmed a hair on his head.

"I know. Come. Let's head downstairs before I lose all thought and drag you back to that bed and really have my wicked way with you." He opened the door and motioned her through.

"That no longer sounds like such a bad thing." She reached up on her toes and kissed his chin then before she could give into the look of hungry need in his eyes, she continued on down the passageway.

They traversed the stairwell then entered the great hall. The massive vaulted room held a sweeping crown of wooden beamed rafters that rose to an impressive height, as well as an impressive number of warriors. A hundred or more were seated at trestle tables stacked with platters of cooked meat, boiled eggs, and bread, all of the men eating their fill as serving maids bustled about offering bowls of hot oats and tankards of warm cider.

At the back table nearest the wide arched stone fireplace where sparks flared and firelight shimmered across the hefty clan shield hanging over it, a good forty MacDonald warriors, a score more than the day before, broke their fast. Since the MacKenzie too desired to take the Chief of MacDonald's land on the Isle of Skye, the MacDonalds had banded together with them in order to fight their enemy as one. Certainly the more warriors they had to defend this keep and the village, the better.

Ahead at the dais, two men sat, both identical to Finlay in every way, from their shoulder-length locks of midnight-black to their wide chests and towering height. Or almost identical. A mark in the shape of a bear's claw graced the neck of the warrior attired in black leather pants and a fur vest over a white tunic. The same mark given to Ivan, Gilleoin's second-born son. The singular claw mark gave proof Ivan's future line would be shifter alone. While, Kenneth, Gilleoin's firstborn son, held the claw-and-star mark symbolizing his dual shifter-fae blood. 'Twas wondrous to see Gilleoin's shifter lines had survived more than eight-hundred years, although now they were on the cusp of extinction and such a loyal line of shifters should never be allowed to fall.

"That's Iain, my eldest brother, with the mark of the claw," Finlay breathed in her ear. "His mate, Isla, sits beside him."

Isla, clothed in a richly colored gown of gold with white silk edging the bodice and cuffs leaned toward Iain, her long brown locks swaying forward. She whispered something then nipped his lobe. He growled, sent her a wickedly hot look that spoke of intended promises then kissed her cheek.

"How long have they been mated?"

"Not long, although it took Iain five years to track her down. She was concerned about joining with him, that she'd lose her own clan, so she ran each night the full moon rose. You would have heard the prophecy your grandmother first spoke of at Kenneth and Ivan's birth, right?"

"Aye, all our clan are aware of it, would never set it aside. 'Twill be told to all future generations, word for word." She slid her hand into his and recited the prophecy. *"Gilleoin's sons will separate when they come of age and rule their own clans, yet there will come a time far in the future when a mated bond forms between the two clans. Only then must Gilleoin's descendants once again merge, and the 'power of three' be unveiled."* She squeezed his fingers. "You and your brothers are the 'power of three.'"

"And you and Isla and now a part of that. The 'power of three' aren't complete without their chosen ones at their sides." He kissed the tip of her nose.

Nessa had often spoken of why the 'power of three' was needed. That if not for them, then in the future, Gilleoin's descendants would be like the leaves that fell from the trees. They would scatter too far and wide then turn to dust, and in doing so, Gilleoin's shifter race would be no more. Only she'd never once imagined she would become a part of it all. As Finlay's mate, there was none other than her to give him bairns, to ensure his line continued to grow from strength to strength. Only how was she to do that when joining with him would ultimately lead to his death? She shuddered with fear.

"What are you thinking?" He stroked the inside of her palm with his thumb, a sweetly gentle caress that sent tingles racing across her skin.

"'Tis naught." She focused on her heat and keeping it contained. Causing a heat wave in front of so many would do nothing but bring about harm. She had to maintain her control.

"That's not the answer I seek." He tugged her into the darkened alcove near the chief's solar where they were assured of a little privacy. "You've nothing to fear by sharing what's in your heart with me. I want to know everything, all that you think, all that worries you."

"I've always wanted bairns, but known I'd never be a mother. I still cannae see how such a thing could be."

"Arabel, you're the one I've been searching for, the one I would never have ceased searching for. There is no other woman for me other than you. I give you my word we'll tackle each coming day together. Good times and bad, we'll always stand by each other's sides."

"I cannae deny these feelings I have for you, the deep need to protect you, although the only way for that to happen is if I let you go afore I no longer can."

A bubbling laugh floated toward her. Isla gazed into Iain's eyes with such a wealth of love. Their bond was strong, but then Isla couldn't kill her mate as she could kill hers.

"Look at me." Finlay planted his hands on the paneled wall either side of her head and leaned in. "From the moment they met, they were inseparable, and Iain desires only Isla's happiness, her safety and wellbeing, just as I desire yours." He surrounded her, his delicious scent wrapping around and comforting her. "We'll find a way around your skill, but you need to keep the faith that we will. They'll be no letting go, for either you or me."

"This is difficult. I never expected to embark on a relationship, particularly one as strong and as all-consuming as the mated bond. You are relentless, and you're also driving me to complete distraction." She grasped his tan shirtfront and tugged him with her into the chief's solar, thankfully devoid of their chief since Gilleoin still remained at the village. The side antechamber held a chunky wooden desk, a tall chest with ornately carved feet and an array of chairs and benches around the perimeter of the room. She halted in the center and said, "Those of us who are fae must uphold ourselves to the sacred laws of our people. There have been six fire-wielders afore me, and the law states that should a fire-wielder cause the death of another through intimacy, then they forfeit their own life. 'Tis a law I will uphold."

"You're my mate, and as I've told you, there isn't a chance you can bring harm to me, just as I can't bring any harm to you. There will be no loss of life, either yours or mine."

"You cannae change who I am, but I assure you, I will protect you, with my dying breath if I must." She leaned in and nipped his lower lip. "This is an impossible bond, one I want, yet I'm completely frightened to embrace."

"We'll embrace all the challenges ahead together, and no matter how impossible our bond appears right now, being with you is all I desire and I'll fight for that right." Grimacing, he scrubbed a hand across his forehead then frowned.

Something brushed against her mind then pushed as if trying to find a way in. Ouch. She rubbed her forehead.

"I'm sorry. That's me. My mind is trying to forge the merged link but is coming up against a solid barrier. A barrier I don't care for."

"Gilleoin and Sorcha have such a merged link. They can speak to each other at will along a pathway known only to them, mind to mind."

"It's a skill inherent in my shifter blood. The fact I'm trying to forge a telepathic link with you is absolute proof you're my chosen one, not that I needed it."

"Can you pull your mind back?"

"Of course." The pain abruptly ceased as he did. "Everything within me desires to be a part of you, Arabel, to speak with you at ease, no matter where you are." He slid one hand around the back of her head and gently drew their foreheads together. His warm breath whispered across her lips. "Has the pain receded?"

"Aye, 'tis gone." She rubbed her forehead against his and her fire once again flared. She twisted out of his hold and paced the room. "My control isnae what it should be and 'tis only getting worse."

"I hate it when you force a separation between us." He growled under his breath but thankfully remained right where he was and didn't bring her back to his side.

"Is everything all right in here?" Kirk strode into the solar in a blue tunic with his clan plaid belted at his waist, sheathed wrist daggers glinting from under his cuffs. He stopped before them, one hand resting on the hilt of his mighty sword as he eyed Finlay. "You and Julia seem to be having a rather intense conversation."

"This isn't Julia but her sister Arabel." Finlay stroked the mark she'd given him on his neck.

"Oh, my apologies, Arabel." Kirk glanced at her. "I wasn't aware you and Julia were twins. She mentioned a sister, but not an identical twin."

"'Tis quite all right. My clansmen mistake us from time to time, as I imagine your kin do with you and your brothers."

"Constantly. It's a never-ending issue." He crossed to the corner padded chair, sat and eyed Finlay. "Last night and this morning I've sensed waves of both contentment and frustration emanating from you. What's going on?"

"I'd like to know the same." Iain walked in with Isla at his side and closed the door behind them. He trod to the desk, moved the quill and ink bottle and perched on the front edge. "It's near impossible to focus with your constant mood changes, Finlay, and I need an answer."

"Then to explain, allow me to introduce you all to my mate." Finlay caught her hand. "Arabel is Julia's sister and Nessa's granddaughter. She also holds the fae skill of fire."

"You're a fire-wielder?" Isla clutched one hand to her mouth. "Fire truly comes forth from your fingertips?"

"Aye, it does." She tugged free from Finlay and crossed to the open window overlooking the inner courtyard. The morning sun beamed through and played over the stack of wood set neatly to the side of the fireplace. She needed to expend this excess of heat roaring through her. She walked to the hearth and lowered to her haunches, her sapphire skirts settling about her. Swiftly, she brought her fire forth and it licked over the wood and chased up the flue.

"That's incredible." Awe crossed Iain's face.

"Her fire is incredible, but it's also very deadly." Compassion filled Isla's eyes as she looked at her. "There have only ever been seven fire-wielders born, and the rare and deadly skill is the only one to ever die out amongst the fae."

"Only seven? Are you sure?" The news sent a shockwave spearing through Arabel, one she couldn't halt. The sudden chill of it penetrated her from the inside out and her cold-fire roared to life.

"I'm certain, and any form of intimacy isn't permitted for a fire-wielder."

"No, that I won't accept." Finlay planted his hands on his hips. "There must be a way to get around her skill."

"I agree." Iain tapped the desk, his gaze narrowed. "The mated bond wouldn't have formed between Finlay and Arabel otherwise. They are a match in every way even though it doesn't appear it."

"I feel cold, very cold." Arabel shivered. Feeling cold was one of the worst signs for one with her skill. Excessive cold-fire, when it generated within a fire-wielder, could take over and kill them from within with its blaze of cold. She rubbed her arms, focused fully on her skill and drew her fire's heat through her in an attempt to curb the cold-fire. 'Twas tricky to get the balance just right and not overexpose herself to her own heat. She must maintain what was required to keep her body and blood warm but not send her hot fire racing through her. Eyes squeezed shut, she attempted to gain back the control she'd lost by the rapid heaving of her emotions. A little hot fire at a time, enough to ground her as she permitted its internal release.

"What's happening?" Finlay crouched in front of her.

"No! Leave her be." Isla seized his arm and pulled him back to his feet. "Finlay, you can't touch her right now. Her cold-fire roars and could take her life. See how she shivers as if with a chill. That is the sign a fire-wielder is consumed by their cold-fire. I've read about it in my clan's history books."

Another surge of cold-fire rose and iced Arabel's fingers and toes. She shook, her lips pinched tight together as she stood once again and faced her mate. "It is as Isla says. When emotions of grief or loss flare too strongly within me then I'm susceptible to certain dangers. Only me. You need no' fear for your own life or those around you when my cold-fire rears." At least her cold-fire couldn't seep from her as the blazing heat of her hot fire could." She nodded at Isla. "Do you hold any information on the last fire-wielder?"

"It's said she passed away during the battle at the village on June the eleventh." Tears filled Isla's eyes and she leaned against Iain's side. "At least that piece of history we can change."

"We'll be changing a hell of a lot more than that." Finlay let out a fierce growl and clenched his fists. His pain and desperation to change what he couldn't tore at her heart. This destructive path he'd embarked on had to change, and she'd ensure it, whether he wished it or not.

"Isla." She glanced at the woman. "As one of my fae kind, you must uphold the sacred laws of our people, and as such, there is something I must ask of you, that I require of your skill."

"Anything."

"I cannae see a resolution to our problem. Finlay and I might be mated, but 'tis a dangerous bond to allow to take. You must compel him to forget me, his brothers too since they appear to stand as one, and if you choose no' to, then I willnae tend to this cold-fire which still consumes me. I certainly willnae be the one to kill my mate, which would happen in only a matter of time since he is so insistent on joining and completing the bond. Killing him isnae an option." She'd been a fool to believe she could be different from the six fire-wielders before her, that it might be possible to have it all, or to at least try and see what would happen.

"Damn it, Arabel." Thumping his chest, Finlay glared at her. He was close, too close, but at least he wasn't touching her. "You are not dying on the eleventh during the battle, or here this very day. Nor are you having me compelled to forget you. You are my mate, and I'll never let you go."

"We'll make sure you don't lose her, Finlay." Kirk grasped Finlay's arm. "We'll keep her safe, all of us, and you too."

"Finlay." She desperately wished to touch him, but since this might be her only chance to ensure his safety, she had to take it. "I cannae burn you, and I have come far too close to doing so already. History has decreed our future and 'tis unchangeable. You need to accept what will be and live as your destiny has proclaimed. You are here to save my fae people in the battle, not me, the last of the fire-wielders. You cannae allow your future shifter clan to fall into extinction. That is where there is hope, not here between us."

"I have no intention of living without you." A fierce rumble left his chest.

Isla sobbed and tears flowed down her cheeks. "Arabel, the last thing I want to do is to take Finlay's chosen one from him. It goes against all that I believe in. The bond is so precious."

"So is his life, which will be very short should he remain with me. Although I must apologize. I've asked you to do something which is unfair. I see that now. The choice to end what is between us will be mine, and mine alone." She would gladly give up her life so he could have his.

Another wave of cold-fire swept through her. The searing cold iced her blood and numb, she shook and fell to her knees. Her heartbeat faltered, lost a beat and made her gasp for breath.

"Arabel, no!" Finlay dropped down beside her, a mere breath away, his anguish tearing through him and her in turn. "Look at me, my sweet. Don't leave me," he pleaded. "If you die, then I die."

"Nessa cannae save the villagers on her own. She needs the 'power of three.'" She lifted one trembling hand to cup his cheek and he jerked back, raw pain slicing across his face as he was forced to do so. "Mated ones dinnae kill each other. You cannae ask me to take your life, because that is surely what will happen."

"You have to believe in us and hold the hope all will be well. There's nothing we can't do if we tackle our issues together."

"You believe in the impossible." And she couldn't, not when his very life hung in the balance. Another wave of loss struck her and her cold-fire continued to consume her. She slumped onto the ground, her pulse so weak and her breathing so labored.

He rose to his feet and shot a look at Isla. "I can't watch her die, and if she lives, at least I'll still have some hope that an answer can be found. Compel us as she's asked."

"Are you sure?"

"There is no other choice. Just make sure my woman warms herself, and don't let her out of your sight until she has. Keep her safe on the eleventh. No one harms her."

"I'll make sure of it." Isla grasped his shoulder and glanced between the three men. "Are you all sure?"

"Aye," Iain said as he moved to stand by Finlay's side. "If Arabel believes that taking her own life is acceptable, then we'll need more time to change her mind, which will be up to you since we'll have no clue what's going on. Compel us."

Kirk too nodded and stepped in beside Finlay. "That goes for me as well. Do what you must, Isla. I trust you."

"I'll do all I can." Her sweetly hypnotic voice rose and flowed through the room. "Finlay, Iain, and Kirk, remain perfectly still and listen to me well. Julia has a twin named Arabel. You'll not recall you've met Arabel before this moment, although you will remain very aware of her deadly skill and the need to take care around her should you come into contact with her. You'll not ponder or think about her overly much. She is no one to you, no more than another woman who resides here within this keep. She is no one of interest or importance. No one to draw too much of your curiosity. You will also not see or acknowledge the mated mark on Finlay's neck. It will be as if gone. Do you hear and understand me?"

"Aye," all three men said, their dazed gazes focused on her.

"Good." She looked deep into Finlay's eyes and murmured, "I'm sorry, Finlay, but no matter how many times you might meet Arabel while we're here in this time, each instance will be as if the first and all other times shall be forgotten." Isla knelt next to Arabel before the fire. "Is there anything more you need me to add which I might have forgotten?"

"Nay. You've covered it all, and I thank you for your aid."

"Then correct your cold-fire, while I'm watching. I won't release Finlay and his brothers from my command until you're back under control."

"Of course." Eyes closed, she focused fully on herself and sent small tendrils of her fire's heat back through her body. Her blood slowly warmed and her control returned, little by little. It took several minutes but once done, heat flushed her cheeks and warmed her fingertips. She lifted her lashes, rose from the ground and nodded at Isla. "'Tis done."

"I wish I hadn't had to do as you asked, but I'll give you fair warning. You must hold the hope as Finlay has asked. Together, we'll do all we can to search for a way for the two of you to be together." Isla hugged her. "You are my sister and I will care for you, just as I care for my mate and his brothers."

"Finlay lives and I live. That is all I can hope for right now, but I too will search for an answer, and if there is one I will grab ahold of it, but if not, then your compelling command on him remains. I willnae take his life." Grief consumed her, beat at her. To keep her cold-fire from returning, she snuck her arms around Finlay's waist where he stood so perfectly still. She nuzzled his neck right over the mark she'd given him, his heavenly scent wrapping around and comforting her. "I will miss you," she murmured against his flesh. "You are my mate and always will be. I'm sorry I forced your hand just now, but there truly was no other choice. You must live and fulfill your destiny. That is all that is important, that the villagers live."

A shuddering breath left his lips.

"You need to go, Arabel." Isla squeezed her arm. "No one has ever broken my compelling command yet, but if anyone could, it would be a man who'd just had his chosen one taken from him."

"Of course." She stepped away and Finlay swayed toward her. Heart shattering, she turned and left.

Chapter 6

Matheson Castle, Scotland, current day.

Murdock Matheson gripped the stone windowsill of his solar on the second floor overlooking the inner courtyard, a fierce vision assailing him.

He couldn't speak to his daughter, but as a seer he saw Isla all the same. She'd compelled Finlay and his brothers and separated the mated pair. His heart ached for Finlay and Arabel and the desperately difficult path they would now tread. Finlay would forever feel incomplete and Murdock knew the feeling well. He'd lost his wife from cancer only a week following Isla's birth. His wife had discovered a lump in her breast during the early stages of her pregnancy and though the doctor had operated, his wife hadn't allowed any further treatment than that, not while she was expecting. She'd given up her life so their daughter could have hers, and her fierce love and devotion for their child had humbled him. Ever since that day, he'd done his best to honor his wife's request of him, to give Isla all the love that she would have given her. And if not for that promise he'd made, he would have gladly taken his own life in order to be with his chosen one. His life was a slow death without his mate, as Finlay's would now be.

"Murdock?"

Nessa's voice jerked his vision toward her. The wise seer of ancient times stood within the fae village along the loch, right near the center well draped in ivy. She wore an elegant olive gown with lacy white sleeves fluttering over her wrists, her red hair wisped with gray coiled high atop her head.

"I see you, Nessa."

"Did you see as I saw? Isla has compelled Finlay and his brothers. I didnae know Finlay and Arabel were mated until this moment, although I have no' seen my granddaughter's death occur at the coming battle as Isla mentioned was recorded in history. Of course I dinnae always see all."

"I never saw my wife's passing either." And for that he'd been most grateful. It would have been sheer hell to know the day and time he would have lost her. "We won't let Arabel die. She's the first with her skill to mate with a shifter and that gives me hope a resolution might be found."

"Aye, and the mated bond wouldn't have formed between Finlay and Arabel unless they were a match in every way. I agree. There is still hope."

"Together, we'll watch over them both."

"We shall. I certainly willnae allow my granddaughter to lose her mated one." A spark of determination flickered in her eyes. "Until the next time, my friend."

"Aye, the next time."

Nessa's image fluttered away, lost to him through the ages, but not the knowledge Nessa would ensure all remained on the right path. She wouldn't fail her people, just as he wouldn't fail them either.

Breathing deep, he cast his gaze out the window. Beyond the breakers, a seagull screeched then circled the foaming waves and dived within. Moments later, it heaved itself out of the water, a flapping fish within its beak as it rejoiced in its victory. It soared along the loch toward the sacred site of the lost village of the fae.

So many lives had been so recklessly lost over eight-hundred years ago, the village leaders so certain they'd never come under attack, but the MacKenzie had wanted it all, and if he couldn't take the House of Clan Matheson and the prized location Gilleoin held at the tip of Loch Alsh, then he'd slaughter them all. Their future had to change.

"Chief." A knock sounded. "It's Daniel."

"Come in." He shook his despondency off as Daniel, his right hand man, walked in and shut the door. "Take a seat."

"Have you *seen* anything more?" In beige pants and a cream muscle t-shirt, Daniel perched on the forest-green couch underneath a wall-hanging of a stunning black and white drawing of Matheson Castle as it had stood in the twelfth century, an image he'd drawn himself from a vision years ago, from the time when he'd first spoken to Nessa through a joint vision.

"Finlay's found his mate, but hit a snag. His chosen one is a woman by the name of Arabel, a woman who also holds the fae skill of fire."

"Ah hell, please tell me you're not serious." Daniel clasped his hands, elbows pressed to his knees. "Being bound to a fire-wielder is a death sentence, for both of them."

"As Arabel is aware. She asked Isla to compel Finlay and his brothers, to ensure that from this moment forth it would be as if she and Finlay had never met. Arabel gave them all very little choice but to agree to her request. If they didn't, she had no intention of tending to her cold-fire that had arisen. She is feisty and strong, and the bond between her and Finlay had clearly taken ahold for her to make such a demand. She desires his protection, even though that means their separation."

"Then all is not lost if they both live." Daniel nodded. "A bond also wouldn't have formed between them unless it was meant to be."

"I agree."

Hope was all their kind needed to survive. Hope brought

courage and desire to the forefront, and allowed their people to be all that they could be. Everything happened within its own time for a reason, and he too would hold hope for Finlay and Arabel. An answer had to be sought. There had to be a way for a fire-wielder to join with their one and only, and if anyone could find it, it would be the 'power of three.'

Chapter 7

Three endlessly long days later, Arabel sat next to Julia at a table at the rear of the great hall to break her fast. She'd been late down to eat, wanting to miss the busy hour following dawn when Finlay and his brothers ate with the other men. Gilleoin, Nessa and Sorcha still remained at the village although Kenneth had returned to oversee the warriors and ensure the teams of men patrolling their borders and the ridge of coastline in and around the keep and the village, were at their most alert.

Julia squeezed her hand, her unwavering presence at her side resolute and unending. Her sister had cried with her when she'd told her of all that had unfolded between her and Finlay, and she'd listened as Julia had told her of her conversation with Nessa. Their grandmother had seen her flares and agreed the four elements had been upset by the arrival of those from the future. Usually realignment was needed, and that occurred when fire, water, air and earth once again joined together as one, something she'd said nature itself had to bring about.

"How is my aura, this morn?" she asked Julia.

"The cold-fire simmers at the edge, but it does no' drift any deeper."

"I'm doing all I can to keep any emotions of grief and loss at bay, but it isnae easy. I miss Finlay. From the moment I left him, I left a piece of my soul behind." She'd snuck as many glimpses of him in during the past three days that she could.

Yesterday, she'd stood at her chamber window as he'd trained below in the yard with the other warriors. His skill with the two-handed claymore was immense. He'd struck the man he'd fought against again and again until his large opponent had wheezed and dropped to his knees under the ferocious onslaught. So too his ability on the archery field surpassed any other. She'd hidden in the forest at the edge of the clearing where the warriors trained. Finlay had swung his bow from his back, eased his left foot slightly in front of the right then slid the arrow into the notch. Only one warrior had hit the target dead center and he'd ribbed Finlay from the sidelines that none could beat him. That hadn't deterred her mate one bit. With fierce determination, he'd lifted the arrow tip and aligned his sight on the red strip of fabric tied around a trunk two-hundred yards away. Then he'd let his arrow go and it had flown free and arched perfectly as it sailed. Right on target, it hit and splintered the other warrior's arrow in two as it embedded itself deep into the trunk.

"Are you all right?" Julia tapped her arm.

"I need to find him. Just being able to see him helps, even though I have to remain out of his sight."

"Finlay is training in the loch, swimming in a loop between here and the village." Julia picked up a small bowl of honey from the center of the table and swirled it over her oats then added a splash of milk from the jug, the ruffled sleeves of her sunshine-yellow gown flapping as she did. She nudged Arabel's spoon toward her. "Come, your oats will go cold if you dinnae eat them."

"I'm no' hungry."

"You still need to eat a spoonful or two." Julia picked up the large pitcher and filled two brass goblets with warm cider, passed one to her and took a sip from the second. "You're to drink as well."

That at least she could do to appease her sister. Brass goblet in hand, she took a sip of the tangy cider then set it back down. Today, just like the last two, the drink slid tastelessly down her throat. Being without her mate tore at her heart, and no matter the smidgeon of hope she clung to, that there might truly be an answer, her despair still rose again and again. Over the last three days, Isla had aided her in scouring through the parchment rolls recording their fae history, papers Nessa kept here within an antechamber off the great hall. They'd sat together for hour upon hour going over all the recordings, yet not once had either of them found anything of use which might lead to a resolution. Even though she'd forced hers and Finlay's separation in order to save his life, if there was a way for them to be together, she intended to find it. Holding even a smidgeon of hope was a powerful thing.

"Arabel?" Julia gasped and shuffled farther away along the bench. "Look at your goblet. There are now indents in the brass, heated indents."

"Is there heat emanating from me?"

"There is. You'll need to visit the pool straight after you've eaten."

"I've already been to the pool, only an hour afore dawn." She'd visited the loch three times yesterday and each dunking had taken longer to cool her adequately. Mayhap she'd never regain her control and she would in fact perish during the battle. Oh well. Better to go out in a blaze of fury aiding her kin than to die for no use at all.

"Cool yourself now with a little water." Julia seized the water jug on the table and set it on the bench seat between them. "Dunk your hands."

She did then waved the steam away. "Is there less heat now?"

"Aye, there is less." Julia's eyes widened on the front door of the keep. "Oh dear. 'Tis Finlay. He shouldnae be done with his swim yet."

Sheathing his sword in his side scabbard, Finlay strode in,

his black hair lying damp and wildly unkempt. Snug rawhide trews of a soft tan encased his muscled legs and a brown leather vest flapped haphazardly over top of his wrinkled white tunic, the hem fluttering free. He slowed at one of the trestle tables several warriors had recently vacated and scanned the hall. She gasped at the sight of the dark circles rimming his eyes.

"Look away," Julia urged her as she stood. "I'm sorry, but it isnae wise to test Isla's compulsion."

"Julia!" Finlay waved out to her sister then strode toward them.

Julia hurried across and grasped his arm and tried to turn him around.

"Is that your sister?" His deep voice sent a thrill racing through Arabel, and needy emotions roared back to insistent life. She drank in the sight of him, unable to do anything less.

"Ah, aye. Arabel is a fire-wielder and you must stay away from her." Julia babbled a bit more then said, "Did you manage to meet the two lasses who returned with their kin from the Isle of Skye last eve?"

"Not as yet. Kenneth informed me they're resting from their journey but should be down before too long. That's why I've returned early from training." His heart-stopping golden gaze traveled over Arabel and she nearly melted onto the floor. Then he marched past her sister toward her. He straddled the bench seat and sat with his knees touching her thigh. "It's nice to meet you, Arabel."

"Tis nice to meet you too, Finlay."

"I've not seen you about the keep since my arrival although your sister has spoken of you." He swept a lock of her hair behind her ear and the sweet gesture had her almost climbing into his lap.

"Finlay, you shouldnae touch Arabel so." Julia pushed his hand away. "She is currently unable to control her skill. There is still heat emanating from her. Can you no' feel it?"

"I can, but my shifter blood runs hotter than most. I can

handle more heat than the usual person. Arabel?" He set his hand on her arm, slid his palm down and curled his fingers around her wrist. "Is there a reason why you can't control your skill?"

"Your arrival caused the four elements to fall out of alignment. Fire, water, air and earth. I now await a realignment for all to return to order."

"For some reason that sounds familiar." He frowned, a glint of confusion in his gaze. "Certainly when we traveled through time, the vortex was strong and hauled us through within mere minutes." His frown deepened. "Your skill must be rare. I've not heard of any other fire-wielders."

"There have only been six born afore me who've held it." Her hand twitched with the need to touch him, just as he touched her. She lifted her hand, cupped his cheek and sighed at the deliciously renewed touch of him. Warmth infused her and she stroked her fingers back and forth over his raspy bristles, her soul soaring. "You need to shave."

"I'm terrible with a blade, always nicking myself." He slid his hand around the back of her head, his fingers firm as he drew her closer. "You have the most glorious silken hair. The color glimmers like gold."

"Arabel was just on her way out. Excuse us." Julia hauled her to her feet. Goodness, her sister was such a pest. "You were going to cool down in the pool. You can talk to Finlay later." She shooed her toward the door. "Go, now, and hurry."

"You'll need a guard, Arabel, even though only to the pool." Finlay stood and tried to dart past Julia but her sister held him back. "It's too dangerous to wander about unescorted, not with the MacKenzie's attack only a few days away. If anything happened to you, I'd never—"

"She'll be perfectly fine on her own." Julia swung him to face her.

Pest or not, she should still do as Julia had said and leave. Grasping her thick red skirts, she backed away and dashed through the door.

Finlay shouted her name and she hastened her step. Too quickly she'd fallen back under his spell, right when she'd gone to such lengths to ensure his safety. She needed to keep a level head, only everything within her cried out for him.

Overhead, heavy gray clouds rumbled in as she hurried across the inner courtyard.

"Arabel, wait." Finlay made chase, his gaze targeted on her.

"I'm sorry. I must leave." She rushed through the gates and into the woods. The branches lining the thin forest trail caught the odd strand of her hair but she rushed on even though he continued to shout for her to halt. No stopping at the pool, or anywhere else he might know. She'd bathe in the pool deep within the underground cavern near the cove. Aye, the cavern was well out of sight and so few knew about it.

Hustling, she broke free of the winding forest path then grabbed a decent breath at the sight of the swampland ahead, a soggy terrain that could bog one down. Slippers kicked off and red skirts rucked high, she squelched across the wetland blooming with the odd marsh orchid, a brilliant burst of fuchsia-pink amongst a stunning array of everglade green. Mother had loved the marsh orchids and Father had always picked her one whenever he'd walked this way.

"I said to wait!" Hands on his hips, Finlay stood at the edge of the forest, his chest heaving as he caught his breath, his gaze on her.

Drat. She hadn't lost him yet. His bear's tracking senses must be strong. She'd have to try harder, move faster, and provided she could escape his sight and his mind, she could get away from him. "Turn back. I dinnae need your aid."

"I can't damn well go back unless you return with me!" He hauled off his boots, tossed them where she'd left her slippers then bounded across the marsh after her, his belted sword swaying at his side. "There's a storm on the way. Can't you see it's closing in?"

Thunder rumbled out at sea and gray clouds above bubbled ominously. "I see the storm just fine."

With her determination strong, she continued to splash through the muddy water, steam curling and rising into the air. He was so close behind, catching up quick.

The wind whistled and whipped her hair about her shoulders as she stumbled free of the marsh and raced along the pebbly stream bank. Thick grass swayed on the other side of the river, all green and lush. She scrambled over the slick boulders and standing on the highest one, breathed deep. This was no idle river, but white water rushing downstream through it from high in the forested hills above. The water flowed around thick gray rocks and streamed around the bend ahead, nature at its most chaotic, the water both a gift and a danger she respected.

She unlaced the front of her corseted gown, shoved the fabric down over her sark and tossed it back onto the dry river bank. She desired a swim, not a drowning, and this river ran for another furlong or two before it gushed into the cove. She'd ride the rapids downstream.

"Don't you dare jump!" Finlay bounded out of the marsh and nabbed her rumpled gown. With the velvet in hand, he flapped it in the air. "Get back here now."

"The water is cold and exactly what I need. You're no' to worry about me. I'm a competent swimmer, very competent." She tucked her sark's ivory hem between her legs and dove. The current shot her to the surface and a rush of water dumped over her head then swelled and sent her bobbing downstream.

A fierce roar echoed. A bear's roar.

She kicked, speeding herself along. Over and over, she was volleyed about and she gulped air holding the heady promise of rain. Thunder boomed all around and lightning slashed the skies, the great spears of gold and white a form of fire she completely adored.

"Woman, when I get ahold of you, you're going to be in the worst kind of trouble." Finlay kicked strongly through the white water toward her.

Goodness. What would it take to get away from him? Ahead, the river twisted into a narrower stream as it met the swirling rush of the incoming tide at the edge of the cove. She grabbed a decent breath then got dumped into the sea. As quickly as she could, she swam toward the white sand beach that curved in a glorious sweep before a jagged rock wall. Exploring the hidden caverns within the cliffs had enthralled her as a child. She adored this place, and always would.

She dragged herself onto the sandy shore and crawled toward the cavern's entrance. So close. Another few feet and she'd be out of his sight and safe again.

"Got you." Finlay scooped her off the ground, water sluicing to his feet, his chest bare and his tan rawhide trews riding low on his hips. "What the hell was that all about? A mad dash through the forest and then deciding you had to risk your life and limb for a swim?"

"I risked naught and you didnae need to follow me. I told you so, repeatedly. You shouldnae be here."

"Where you are is where I need to be." Confusion lit his gaze before he tipped his head toward the entrance. Lightning crackled overhead and the waves pounded into shore. "At least we'll be able to seek shelter out of the rage of the storm here. That tunnel must lead somewhere."

"It leads to an underground cavern. There's a cold pool within. That's where I need to swim in order to cool my fire."

"You're already drenched, and you feel cold, not hot at all. I believe you've doused any fire that arose earlier just fine." He strode through the opening as the wind rushed around them. With a purposeful step, he carried her down the darkened, precariously wet tunnel carved of stone, leapt from the end of the passageway and landed with a soft thump on the grainy white sand a few feet below. Water lapped onto a small curved beach surrounded by massive black rocks.

"This place is incredible. I had no idea this was here." His stunned gaze moved upward to the craggy ceiling where a thin shaft vented skyward and allowed a trickle of light to beam through the tiny cavity and wash over the pool's darkened surface.

"There's another pool on the other side of that ledge, farther along the tunnel. It holds hot water while this one is cold. My parents and Julia always swam in the heated one while I favored the cold pool."

"Where are your parents now?" He set her on her feet, kept one finger under her chin as he looked into her eyes.

"They were slaughtered by the MacKenzie a couple of years ago." Her grief rose, as it always did when speaking of her parents.

"I'm so sorry." He hauled her into his arms, brushed a kiss across the top of her head. "No one should have to lose their parents, particularly at another's hand. Can you speak of it at all?"

The need to ensure he knew all about her again resounded strongly within her and the words burst forth. "My father wished to arrange Julia's marriage. She was set to wed the Chief of MacKenzie's third son and when the MacKenzie requested a meeting, we discovered 'twas naught but a ruse. As soon as they arrived at the MacKenzie's stronghold, he had them tossed into his dungeon and then a demand sent to Gilleoin. My uncle was told to hand over his lands on the tip of Loch Alsh and in return the MacKenzie would release my parents."

"He didn't release them?" He stroked her back and she held onto him, slid her thumbs inside his waistband and curled her fingers around his trim waist.

"Nay. Demands volleyed back and forth until Gilleoin set out for the MacKenzie's castle. He took an elite team of warriors with him, men who could move swiftly under the cover of darkness and they successfully slipped inside the keep. Only after they arrived, Gilleoin discovered my parents had already been slain several months afore, and at the MacKenzie's own hand. He was furious and he attacked with great force then left a bloody trail in his wake. That is why the MacKenzie is so determined to have his retribution, to ensure he takes all Gilleoin holds dear."

"And why he will soon strike at the very heart of clan Matheson." Retribution blazed in his gaze. "My brothers and I will never allow the MacKenzie to take the fae village. Of that I give you my word."

"I know. You and your brothers are the 'power of three' and your arrival means the world to us." She needed to let him go, had taken more time with him than she should have. Stepping back, she wrapped her arms around her damp body. Her sark was still wet. Unusual. She usually dried it with barely a thought. She turned her hands palms up and focused on bringing heat to them, only not even a glimmer of her fire rose.

"What's wrong?" Finlay followed her. "I don't care for the distance you're creating between us."

"My fire. It's gone." She walked into the water and shoved her hands under the surface. No steam. She straightened and once again tried to find the well of heat deep inside her and bring it back to glorious life, but nothing happened. She couldn't even raise a flicker of flame.

"Has this happened before?" He crowded her from behind, pressed his chest against her back, all solid heat and hard muscle.

"Never."

"Is this a good thing or bad?" He slid one hand around her waist and with his other hand, swept her hair from her neck and exposed her neck. He nuzzled her flesh, his wet hair sliding across the top of her shoulders as he did. "I'm sorry, Arabel, but I can't seem to control myself around you. The need to touch you is strong."

"I love your touch." No fire meant she couldn't harm him. She reached back, cupped the back of his head and held his mouth against her neck. Heat curled low between her thighs, and not the heat of her skill. This was the heat of passion and she couldn't help but embrace it.

"My bear is intrigued by you, and so am I." He razzed his teeth back and forth over her sensitive flesh then nibbled up to her ear and back. "I'm searching for my mate, and she is one of the fae."

"I'm aware." Need rushed through her and she slowly turned around. She threaded her fingers deep into his hair and guided his mouth to hers. She kissed him, with all the longing she held deep within her heart and hadn't allowed to release in three long days. Except having his warm lips on hers and the hard length of his body plastered against her only fueled her need for more. More she desperately wanted to take. "I love the feel of your mouth on mine."

"I've never felt this kind of desire for any other woman, not once, not ever." A low growl rumbled within his chest. "You don't mind kissing me?"

"I want far more than your kisses while the chance has arisen. My heart is beating so fast." She wanted this moment even though he remained under Isla's compulsion. He'd never recall anything once they parted ways, but he'd told her to hold onto hope and she damn well intended to. This was the first time she'd ever exhausted her fire and she intended to take full advantage of it.

She pressed her breasts against the wicked heat of his chest and ran her thumb over the fading mark she'd left on his neck. Her mouth watered with the need to bite him again, to bring that mark back to brilliant life and she leaned in and sucked his skin deep into her mouth then teeth firm, bit down, hard enough to leave a mark, just as she desired.

He lifted his head high and roared. Fur rippled across his chest and down his arms, a soft padding that was there one moment and gone the next.

"Do you need to shift?" She stepped back and he stepped forward, closing the distance between them as quickly as she'd instilled it.

"No, what I need to do is kiss you."

"I like your kisses." She stroked his shoulders and arms, so thick and strong and below the planes of his wide chest, his abs rippled, layer upon tight layer. She itched to touch more of him while her fire was doused, to run her fingers through the delicious tease of dark hair narrowing down his rigid belly and disappearing into his trews. Sweet heaven. She needed all the kisses he could give her right now, and with no delay. She ran her thumb across his warm lips and a little breathless, murmured, "May I touch more of you, just to make sure my fire has truly gone?"

"If you wish to touch me, then I'm all yours." He caught her hands, pressed them against his chest. "Touch me wherever and however you please."

"If you feel my heat, even the slightest flicker, then tell me, right away. Promise me."

"I promise."

She dragged in a deep breath and let her hands wander. She caressed down his chest, trailed one finger along the hard ridges of his abs then cupped his hips. Could she go further? Once, when she'd been out wandering in the woods, she'd stumbled upon a warrior and lass coupling. Shock had initially halted her step, then the knowledge she'd never experience such a joining had kept her rooted there. She'd ducked in behind a bush as the lass, on her knees before the warrior, hauled his trews down and covered his shaft with her mouth. He'd adored the attention, grunting and groaning before toppling the lass to the ground then rucking up her kirtle's skirts. His head had disappeared under the layers of brown linen and the woman's eyes had near rolled to the back of her head as pleasure had consumed her. It hadn't taken long before the lass thrashed her head from side to side and the man lifted free of her, licked his lips in hearty appreciation then thrust his cock inside her. They'd come together in a loud and boisterous cry. That's what she wanted. To take this stolen moment in time and claim it for them both.

"Do you still feel no heat?" She caressed his sides.

"Not a flicker of heat. That I promise you."

"Finlay, what would you say if I asked you to bite me?"

"A shifter only allows the bite and touch of his mate, as his mate can only allow the same." He walked her farther backward into the water, until her sark twisted around her legs and she had to seize his arms to keep from toppling over. "I allowed your bite for a reason, Arabel. You are my chosen one."

"So that's an aye?"

"It is, but I desire to do far more than bite you. We're mated, and that I can sense to the depths of my soul." He dipped his head and kissed her, so surely and with such breathless urgency.

Lost, she kissed him back and allowed herself to get caught up in his powerful embrace. Aye, they were mated and she couldn't let him go, not now, not when she finally had a chance to claim him. Hope. It had now fluttered to vivid life in her chest and wouldn't let go.

* * * *

Hunger for the woman before him consumed Finlay. When he'd first seen Arabel this morning in the great hall, her presence had nearly knocked his breath from his lungs. He'd known Julia had a twin who held the skill of fire, a dangerous ability, but something about this woman drew him directly toward her, made him long to touch her, to have her look at him with those beautiful blue eyes rimmed with sparks of gold. For three days he'd tossed and turned at night, his bear raging for release and his heart twisting in on itself. Fleeting images of a pool of water rippling under a moonlit sky had tormented him. Something had happened there, something important, but he couldn't hold onto the memory before it was wrenched painfully away.

Now, all that torment had eased and this moment took precedence. Arabel was his and his bear had fought hard to track her down and keep her in his sight.

Kissing her deeply, he drank in her essence, devouring her. He had to make her his, to complete the bond and tie her to him, for now and for all time, while her skill lay dormant. The knowledge rode him hard, was impossible to ignore. Hope. There was hope.

He broke their kiss, looked deep into her eyes. "I want the right to touch you, as freely as any man does with his woman."

"I want that too."

"Once we join, you'll be mine, just as I'll be yours." He traced one finger along the low-cut neckline of her shift where the upper swells of her breasts rose. Her nipples beaded and poked the cloth, the fabric wet and molding her full breasts. Those nipples were juicy morsels he couldn't wait to taste. He scooped her up, pushed through the water with her in his arms toward the ledge that ran along each side of the pool and sat her on top of the chiseled rock. Water sluiced down her legs and dripped into the pool.

After hauling himself up beside her, he stood and lifted her to her feet then led her along the ledge and deeper into the darkened rear where a shower of fresh water sprayed into the cavern between two cracks high in the rock wall. She might have exhausted her fire, but he wouldn't take any unnecessary risks, not when she worried so greatly about hurting him.

"This is perfect." She stepped under the spray and with a giggle, twirled around. The water plastered her already wet shift to every curve of her body, outlining her trim waist and slim legs.

Hell, he couldn't wait to strip that garment from her.

"It's been far too long since I was last here." She wrapped her arms around his neck, reached up on her toes and kissed his chin.

"You missed my lips by an inch."

"Then bend a little."

He swooped down, claimed her lips and kissed her as the spray covered them both. Breath melded with hers, his desire to complete the bond with his mate pulsed through him. "Since I arrived in this time, I've searched for you each and every day, and would never have given up. From this moment forth, we will be as one. Never will I be parted from you again."

"You are the only one I want, always and forever."

"I want to make love to you, to bury myself so deeply inside you that neither of us will know where one ends and the other begins." Slowly, he skimmed her sides, stroked around to her bottom and brought her hard up against him. Sensations stormed through him. His heartbeat pounded. His blood rushed, hot and needy. His fingers twitched to touch more of her, and his tongue ached to taste.

"That is what I desire too." A breathy answer, and all he needed to hear.

"Then let me do this right." She wasn't from the future, her time here quite different to his own. He removed the leather tie at the waist of his tan pants, clasped his right hand with her right and wrapped the thin strip of rawhide around both their wrists. The symbolic gesture brought all his protective urges to the forefront. "So there is no misunderstanding about our bond, I wish a handfast. Bind yourself to me as my wife for a year and a day, and before that time has passed, I'll ensure we're wed proper before our clans."

"Are you certain?"

"Your fire has been exhausted, and we'll find a way to exhaust it again, and as often as we can." Finding an answer to do so would consume him. "You must hold the hope and faith that we will."

"I will. You have my word I will." Delight flared in her blue eyes. "I dinnae wish to lose this one precious moment. I've dreamed of being with you."

"How is that since we just met?"

"Never mind." She kissed him and his question flittered from his mind. "Is there to be a handfast?"

"There is." He lowered to his knees, caught her hands and brought them to his lips. "Speak vows with me, Arabel. There is no other I'll ever desire than you. I'll begin." He cleared his throat. "I, Finlay Michael Matheson, of Ivanson Castle, pledge my troth to Arabel, of the House of Clan Matheson. With this handfast, I take her as my wife for the next year and a day, and as my mate for all time." He tightened his grip on her hand. "I want you as mine, in every single way."

"As I want you. I cannae believe I am going to handfast with you." She sank to her knees, her fingers twined with his. "I, Arabel, of the House of Clan Matheson, pledge my troth to Finlay Michael Matheson. With this handfast, I take him as my husband for the next year and a day, and as my mate for all time." She stared at the leather around their wrists and smiled as she raised her gaze back to his. "My parents would have adored you for doing this."

"As I adore you, my wife and my mate. Now we seal the vows with a kiss." He captured her mouth and kissed her, until her soft body swayed forward and embedded his with a fierce heat that had nothing to do with her skill. His need to join with her increased tenfold, although his need to ensure she reached the heights of pleasure before he entered her, even more so. "Whatever you need from me, you'll speak it. I want to know what you like, or what you don't like. What you'd prefer for me to do, or not do."

"I want to experience everything you can offer, while it's possible for me to receive it, to be with you in every way, but if I sense my skill is reigniting then we stop, without question."

"Of course. Safety comes first." He tugged the leather strip binding their wrists free then rose to his feet and drew her to hers. "I'm going to remove your shift. Is that acceptable?"

"Very, provided you also remove your trews."

"You've got a deal, but your clothing first." He crouched, gripped her hem and lifted the fabric. He exposed her body to his hungry gaze, inch by incredible inch. Enticing calves, sweetly curving inner thighs, and a thatch of golden curls covering her mound. He breathed her honeyed scent deep into his lungs, his bear clawing at him as he did. Aye, everything about her called to him, as if she were a piece of his soul and he'd found her again.

"Finlay?" She swayed, braced her back against the rock wall, her palms flattened to its slick, sheer surface either side of her.

"Aye, what do you need?"

The spray showering through the rock misted over her and she licked her wet lips as she smiled at him. "Just you, all of you."

"As I need you." Arabel was all he'd ever hoped for in a mate. Feisty and strong, his match in every way. Now, he had her all to himself and he didn't intend to allow one inch of her body to go untouched, not by his hands or his tongue. He peeled her shift up, over her flat belly and higher until the undersides of her breasts were exposed. His cock filled and lengthened, the head escaping his loosened waistband and poking out. "Hands up, my mate."

She lifted them and he swept her shift over her head and exposed all of her.

"Hell, you're so beautiful." Her creamy skin beckoned and he trailed one finger down her neck and between the valley of her breasts until she arched her back and thrust her breasts out farther. Accepting the offering, he cupped their fullness, weighed them in his hands then eased them together and swiped his thumbs over her beaded nipples. So wet and shiny and hard under the cool, freshwater spray. He licked one nipple then the other and when she whimpered and her knees buckled, he caught her and lowered her to the ground on top of her shift.

"Trews off," she whispered, the heated look in her eyes capturing his gaze.

"Aye, whatever you ask, I shall do." He gripped his loosened waistband and shoved his leather pants down his legs and off. He tucked the leather underneath her, adding another layer of cushioning between her and the rock, his cock brushing her belly as he knelt between her spread legs.

Tentatively, she touched the head of his cock, swirled one finger along the slit and caught the drop of pre-come on the tip. She brought it to her lips, within an inch before the spray misting over them washed it away. Smiling, she gazed at him. "I never thought this moment would be possible, that I would be able to touch you so freely, that you and I might lie like this together. I still cannae raise any fire. None will come forth at all. Such a miracle, one I intend to take complete advantage of, and then discover how it occurred. This has never happened to a fire-wielder afore."

He couldn't deny the depth of their bond already roaring to glorious life. It was as if he already knew her, as if his soul had connected with hers and claimed her at some other time.

"Finlay?" She reached between them, gently cupped his balls with one hand and wrapped her fingers around his shaft with the other, her actions scattering his thoughts once again. "I am yours."

"Aye, as I am yours." He leaned in and kissed her, sucked her tongue between his lips and nibbled on her. She moaned into his mouth, tightened her grip on his cock and softly massaged his balls. She had the most exquisite touch, as if she was attuned with his body and knew exactly where he ached for her. His cock hardened further, pulsing with a throb from root to base that warned him he'd need to back off soon or else come before he'd even begun. He eased away, lost the delicious hold of her hands on him but gained her entire body as a platter to be gorged upon. And gorge he would. He couldn't wait to sample all her sweet body offered. His. Always, his.

Chapter 8

Arabel lost her luscious grip on Finlay's cock as he eased back and swept his burning gaze over her body. She should be nervous, but that emotion hadn't once flickered through her. Amazement and desire had taken ahold of her since they'd entered this cavern and wouldn't let go. Then from the moment Finlay had removed her sark, eased her breasts together and licked her sensitive nipples, a bolt a pleasure had coursed through her and a liquid heat had invaded her core, one fiery burn unlike anything she'd ever experienced before.

Could this really be happening? Could she complete the bond and join with him in all ways? He'd spoken vows with her, made her his handfast wife and she'd honor her vow to him, even if she only had this one moment in time to join with him. She would remain his and cherish this memory forever.

Exquisite sensations stormed through her and she sighed with a smile as Finlay knelt between her legs, his balls drawing tighter and higher into a thatch of black curls covering the apex of his groin. She feasted her gaze on every inch of him, took in his muscled thighs and his shaft as it brushed his belly, one very large cock with a plump head darkening to a ripe raspberry color. Mere moments ago, she'd palmed his balls and caressed his smooth skin, swiped a bead of his essence from the tip and almost tasted it before the mist spraying over them had stolen the treasure from her. How she wanted to take him in her mouth, just as the serving lass had done with the warrior when they'd coupled.

"What are you thinking, my sweet?" He raised her knees, flexed his fingers on top, his claws slicing out then retracting. "Because that hungry look in your eyes is making me very hard. My bear is greedy for everything, has waited a long time to find and claim you."

"I ache for whatever you can offer me." She lifted her hands to the spray, allowed the cool mist to coat her entire body. Relief poured through her. Still no fire, not even one whiff of it. She giggled, having never known such delight. She was normal, not a danger to a single soul, or at least right in this moment she wasn't. Aye, she could touch Finlay and know she couldn't burn him, share her body with him and not harm a hair on his head, take him deep inside her and be as one, just as they both desired. This was a dream come true, one she didn't wish to miss a moment of. She eased up a little and traced the ridged bands of his stomach. His hard muscles were honed to perfection, and his abs, they rippled as she brushed the head of his cock, fondled the tip and glided to the root. "You feel so hard, yet your skin is smooth like velvet."

He hardened further and groaned. "I love how you touch me, and the freedom you take in doing so. I never want that to change. I need to feel your hands on me. Wherever you please."

"You dinnae think I'm too forward?" She couldn't be anything else if she didn't want their time together here to be lost.

"Never. I'm most grateful you're not frightened of what's about to happen between us." He leaned forward, touched his forehead to hers. "I do need to warn you though. With our joining, comes the merging of our minds. My shifter blood will demand a telepathic link, and my mind will tunnel into yours and find a pathway that is just for us. From this moment forth, you'll be able to touch my mind at will, whenever you please, no matter the distance separating us, just as I will be able to do the same with you."

A link she wanted, but also a link that would cause one glaring problem considering the compelling command upon him. "There is no way around it?"

"None whatsoever, and I can't wait for that moment when our minds merge." He grinned, toppled her back onto the soft bedding of his trews and kissed her, his tongue sweeping over hers then delving deep. A surge of desire flooded her and an ache pulsed between her thighs. All her thoughts scattered as Finlay scented the air and let out a low moan.

"You smell incredible. Like sweet, sweet honey. It's heady, a taste I want to smother myself in. I need more." He kissed her again, so deliciously he turned the heat radiating through her blood into a roaring fire, until every inch of her sizzled, until her heartbeat thumped like thunder in her ears. She needed this, needed him. She'd deal with the merged link of the mind later, as well as the compulsion upon him. Nothing mattered at this moment but their joining. She had to grab ahold of that while she could.

Rising into his touch, she pressed her breasts to his chest and rubbed the achy tips against him. He swept his hands over her ribcage, fastened his sight on her breasts then bent his head and licked first one nipple and then the other. Nice and slow. Real slow. So good. Then he razzed his teeth over one sensitive tip, taking a second before drawing the aureole deep inside his mouth. He sucked. Hard. Sweet heaven. Never had she known such sheer pleasure. His attentions made her toes tingle and when he tweaked her other nipple, she arched her back and pleaded for more.

He delivered, easing both her breasts together and gorging, kissing and licking, taking her nipples between his lips and rolling his tongue around them before nipping. His little bites, each a claiming, intensified their bond and pulled her heart and soul closer toward his.

Hips pushing into him, she clutched his broad shoulders, traced over his roped biceps and down his arms. So wickedly strong. More. She stroked his firm back and tapered waist, cupped his butt, which tightened in her hands and made her smile giddily.

Surrounding her, his delectable fresh scent wrapping around her, he dipped his fingers between them and glided along the inside of her thigh. Her legs trembled and her core became bathed in heat. "Tell me to touch you deep inside," he whispered in her ear. "I need to hear that you wish for this joining as greatly as I wish for it."

"Aye, I want all of you, touching all of me." Craving what he too needed, she eased her legs apart, so wantonly. She couldn't halt this moment any more than he could. "Dinnae stop, Finlay. Your thoughts shall become my thoughts, your passion my passion."

"You still feel no heat rising?" He swept his hand over her entrance, his intimate touch scalding her, but only in the way of her rising passion.

"There is none."

"Then this day, we shall be one." Looking into her eyes, he plunged one finger inside her, stroked deep then curled his finger into a spot that had her arching her back. He breathed deep then grinned with a hungry growl. "Your body is crying out for mine. I can almost taste you on my tongue." He licked her lower lip, sucked it into his mouth then released her. "I've got to taste the rest of you. I can't wait any longer."

Head bent, he kissed down her body to where his finger played then nibbled along her inner thighs, his breath hot on her skin as he rubbed her nub.

She bucked as he stroked, harder and faster, then clutched his head as he spread her legs even wider. She moaned, long and low as he parted her folds and licked her flesh in the most intimate way. Every flick of his tongue over her nub was such exquisite torture, and watching him lave such attention on her, increased her pleasure to the point of pain. He sucked and her core pulsed as wave after wave of pure bliss rocked through her. She soared and a stunning display of bright colors burst behind her closed eyelids.

"I need to be inside you, now." He crawled up her body, his mind battering against hers, demanding entrance.

"Be mine, Finlay, always mine." She wrapped her legs around his waist as he set his hands on her hips and slowly, carefully, moved between her legs and nudged his cock along her slick folds.

"I'll always be yours." His mind shoved against the barrier still between their minds and he groaned, a look of anguish crossing his face. "I don't wish to hurt you."

"It will hurt more if you dinnae join with me. Do it. This could be our only chance." She cupped his butt and rocked underneath him. It was all the incentive he needed. He plunged, tore through her barrier below, just as his mind barreled into hers. He joined them together in all ways, mind, body and soul.

Never had she been laid so completely bare and open. His mind tunneled deep inside hers, creating a private pathway that would only ever be theirs. Such a beautiful connection. She grappled to cement the link and whispered into his mind, "*My warrior, my lover, the other half of my soul.*"

"*Aye, and we shall never be parted again.*"

"*I feel so wonderfully full.*" Her heart and body verged on bursting with how full she felt.

"*I feel whole, as if I can finally rest and know my search is done, yet with your sweet body hugging mine, I'm also about to careen right over the edge of reason.*" Ever so slowly, he slid back out then halted and with a low moan, pushed all the way back inside her. "*I want to make you come, over and over, and to share in all you feel. Keep your mind open to mine.*"

She did as he bid and clung to him, her arms wrapped tightly around his neck and her legs firm around his hips. "*This time we come together.*"

"Aye, together." He thrust, pounding into her and as he did, he sucked the skin of her neck between his lips.

"Are you going to bite me?"

"Hell, yes." One very territorial growl.

"Then I'm biting you too." She rocked with him as he moved, scraped her teeth over the fiercely beating pulse in his neck and when she could hold on no longer, she marked him, as possessively as any woman could mark her man. Her mate. Her bear.

"Do that again," he demanded as he plunged into her, over and over, his pace wildly fervent.

She bucked, her heartbeat a pounding mess against his but she reveled in the moment, bit down and marked him. He roared his pleasure, then he bit her and sent every one of her last thoughts flying. She cried out his name, his bite pure passion and a temptation she would crave until the end of her days. Her channel tightened, squeezed his cock and dragged him even deeper inside her. His seed pulsed from him in one long hot rush, coating her womb and her heart soared right along with her soul. She wanted this, all of him, throughout all of time. She couldn't give him up a second time. Not now. She would hold onto the hope that had bloomed and never let it go. Their mated bond was meant to be, that she now knew to the depths of her heart. Finlay had been right. No one could halt the mated bond. Not even her.

* * * *

Finlay's mind went dark with lust and a powerful whirlpool of need surged. Desperation and passion slammed through him and with her pulse skittering out of time under his lips, he sank his teeth into her flesh a second time and roared as he thrust balls-deep inside her.

She continued to convulse around him, crying out his name as she rode the waves right along with him. His essence streamed into her, his mind and body locked tight around hers as he joined them fully as one. Never could he have imagined a more perfect moment, and this was just the beginning.

He kissed her, stroking her sides as he slowed his pace and rocked gently inside her. With a tender touch, he eased up on his elbows and carefully brought them both back down.

She stretched, her beautiful breasts on full display and tempting him almost beyond his endurance. She was so alluring with her creamy skin, luscious lips that pouted so perfectly, and long slender neck now bearing his mark. He licked the outline of his bite and purred.

"Mmm," she murmured and caught his face between her hands. She kissed him, so sweetly and seductively his cock stirred back to vibrant life and twitched again inside her. Grinning, she licked her lips. "By the feel of you hardening once more, I believe it might be time for us to do that all over again."

"I need to take care of you first." He was driven to ensure her welfare and he eased out, tipped her over onto her front and smoothed his hand down her back and over her bottom. No scrapes but her flesh appeared a little pink. Thankfully, her shift and his pants had protected her from the stone.

Smiling wickedly, she glanced over her shoulder at him, her wet blond locks sliding forward as she wriggled up onto her hands and knees. The spray continued to coat her slick flesh and there, along her inner thigh sat a streak of blood that made his bear growl with approval. She'd gifted him with her innocence, just as he'd gifted her with his. He leaned over the side of the ledge, scooped handfuls of water and gently washed her clean then splashed his cock.

She wriggled even more, elongating her neck and body as if enjoying every drop of cool water on her skin. Slowly, she inched around and faced him, her breasts swaying heavy and full as she pushed him onto his back and crawled over top of him. She sat across his hips and lifted her arms high. Water trickled down her body, over her pebbled nipples, her flat belly and down into the thatch of golden curls covering her mound. "Can you hear the storm still raging outside?"

High above their sanctuary hidden deep within the earth, thunder rumbled in the skies. A flicker of lightning lit the chamber through the vent and wind rushed down the tunnel and swirled around them. "The four elements have come together, fire, water, air and earth. It is a mighty storm."

"The realignment." She gasped and grinned. "'Tis just what I needed to restore my control following the disruption caused by your arrival. My grandmother said nature itself had to bring it about. I wonder if the realignment is what has extinguished my fire?" She wriggled against his groin, rubbing her slit over the base of his cock wedged between them. "Oh, I like this position. Sitting on top of you is rather wicked."

"Take care. You must be sore." He grazed a finger from between her breasts to her belly, and as her breath caught, he trailed lower, swirling through her curls and over her clit.

She jumped, caught his hand and smiled. "There is a tingle. I'm sensitive from so much pleasure and yet I also desire more, but mayhap in a little while, after I've had my turn with you. There are things I wish to do." She squirmed back and rested on her belly between his legs, her breasts falling gently either side of his balls as she curled one hand around his stiff cock. "I have an admission to make. I once stumbled upon a couple in the woods, and well, I wish to love you in the way I saw them love each other, with her mouth upon him. If you will allow it?"

Oh hell. If she took him in her mouth right now, he'd likely lose it. Yet the look of hope in her eyes wasn't one he intended to snuff out.

Through long lashes, she peeked at him, one brow raised. "Will that be permissible?"

"Look into my mind and you'll see the answer you seek." He opened his thoughts for her to read, sharing exactly what just raced through his mind. He'd experience only sheer pleasure if she did such a thing.

"I like being in your mind." She grinned and dipped her head, and in one long teasing stroke, licked him from root to tip then swirled over the head.

Pleasure spiraled through him and he groaned and clenched his butt. A bead of come leaked and she ogled the drop glistening on the end before quickly cupping one palm like a shield over it to shelter it from the spray above.

"This is for me?" She looked into his eyes, such desire flaring in her own.

"If you wish it." He cradled her head in his hands, his cock hardening impossibly further.

"Oh, I wish it." She rimmed his head with her mouth, took him deep and caressed his balls and his shaft. She bobbed up and down on him, finding a rhythm that would send him mad in no time at all.

Heat shimmered at the base of his spine and radiated out to curl his toes. "Arabel, my sweet, you must have watched that couple in the woods with dedicated attention."

"Aye, and glad I am that I did. You are delicious and I desire more. This is a treat I wouldnae have wished to miss out on." She sucked harder and he pushed himself deeper inside her mouth. He got lost as a sexual haze consumed him, as red flared behind his eyes. No, he needed to maintain his control. He wouldn't allow himself to come until he'd seen to her pleasure again. She deserved all he could possibly give her, every single part of him.

Gripping her waist, he lifted her up onto her hands and knees, scooted down under her on his back and planted his head between her thighs. Her inner flesh lay plump and pink, an enticement he couldn't resist. He licked her, again and again, then captured her clit gently between his lips and rolled his tongue around her. She half-moaned, half-sighed then shuddered, her legs trembling and barely holding her up.

He gave her no relief. Blood pounding, he lavished attention on her, until she rocked her hips and cried out, "Mercy. I feel too much, too hot."

"Your fire?" He sensed no heat coming from her, her skin the same warmth as his and the spray falling on them not heating or hissing at contact. He tweaked her hard nipples and she gasped.

"No fire," she panted. "I need you inside me."

"I'm coming, love." He wriggled out, crawled over top of her hand-and-knees position and crowded her from behind, the heat of her back against his chest sublime. His bear growled for dominance, that he mark his woman again. He opened her folds and stroked her wet slit. In her ear, he whispered, "Do you want me?"

"I want my mate. I want all of you."

"I want you too." He clasped her hips, pushed his cock between her legs and before she could draw her next breath, he plunged deep inside her heavenly warmth.

"Finlay." She cried out his name, pushed her bottom back into his groin and met each and every one of his thrusts. She urged him on, her breathing and his loud in his ears, her inner muscles locking tight around him as he rocked into her, his balls slapping the insides of her thighs. "Please, bite—"

He sank his teeth into her neck and she gasped and squeezed him harder.

"More, again," she demanded.

He moved to the other side of her neck, swept her hair away and laying his claim so completely, bit her again.

"Oh, your bite is sheer heaven. 'Tis an aphrodisiac, just as you said." Her pleasure radiated down their link as she pulsed around him, wrapped him in her body's blaze of heat and sent him soaring right along with her.

Completely spent, they collapsed onto their clothing, his body blanketing her back.

"When did I say that?" he murmured when his thoughts came back under control. "About our bite being an aphrodisiac?"

"Mmm." Her word a breathy whisper from her lips before

she whispered in his mind, *"I love you, Finlay, so much my heart can barely contain all that I feel for you. You hold my very soul in your hands, and always will."*

Her declaration humbled him and he opened his heart and tucked her words deep inside. She wasn't just his mate, not now. She was his only reason for living, the one person he could never survive without, his entire heart and soul. *"There is none,"* he said along their link as he kissed her cheek, *"who I will ever love as greatly as I love you. My wife, my lover, and the other half of my soul."*

"You're also heavy." She smiled as she glanced over her shoulder at him. *"So beautifully heavy."*

He rolled onto his side and tucked her safely within his arms.

Her eyelids fluttered down and he relaxed and allowed his own exhaustion to take him under. It was as if he'd known her his entire life, as if he'd been waiting for her to return to him. She was his match in every way, all he could have ever desired in a mate. His. Always his.

Chapter 9

The hoot of an owl and the sloshing of waves drifted into the cavern from outside and Arabel stirred from her sleep. She opened her eyes and stretched under the cool mist while overhead a trickle of moonlight slithered through the vent and played over the pool's glassy, darkened surface.

She wriggled around and smiled as her mate still slept so soundly, his big body cocooned warmly around hers. Gently, she touched the two adorable dimples either side of his luscious lips then tucked back the charming lock of silky black hair curling onto his forehead. The mist beaded over his golden skin, every single naked and superb inch of him.

Oh, how she wanted to stay with him forever, right here in this magical place. But to do that, she first needed to fix so many things. His compulsion still stood, and although they'd joined, he'd never remember it the moment they parted ways. So too she needed to consider the realignment of the elements that had exhausted her fire, the lightning that had flashed through the vent above, the wind that had rushed down the tunnel, the water misting over them, and their cavern itself deep within the earth. The four elements had come together and a miracle had happened. Although this exhaustion of her skill better not be just a one-time thing, only occurring because of the realignment being needed. Certainly no fire-wielder had every managed an intimacy on the level she just had, an intimacy she needed again, well just as soon as she'd fixed everything she'd set moving on the wrong path.

I'll make things right, Finlay. That I promise you, but for now, I must go. Words she kept to herself even as she wanted to speak them out loud.

Carefully, she extricated herself from Finlay's hold, wiggled her scrunched sark still half caught underneath him out then slipped it over her head. She would never give up the hope that they could make this work, not now she'd experienced what it was like to be in his arms. That kind of heaven she could never live without.

On soundless feet, she tiptoed to the end of the ledge then hopped from boulder to boulder until she reached the beach and jumped onto the sand. Swiftly, she clambered through the darkened tunnel of carved stone and hurried out onto the sandy beach of the cove. Under the clear moonlit sky twinkling with stars, the sea's white-tipped waves rolled gently into shore. She lifted her hands and turned them palms up and tried to bring forth her fire. A touch of heat tingled her fingertips, but no flames yet flickered to life. Her skill was returning now the lightning and wind had settled. She sensed that deep within her. The four elements had now been dispersed.

She strode toward the river mouth where the water flowed smoothly into the sea. She splashed through then blew a kiss toward the cavern's entrance. As she did, she searched along her merged link and touched Finlay's mind. He remained blissfully asleep. She closed their link, her determination strong. She'd right the wrongs she'd done and she wouldn't rest until she had.

She continued on, walking back along the river's edge until she reached the place where she'd first jumped in. The waning moonlight beamed over her drenched gown caught between two boulders and she wriggled it free. A little more warmth seeped from her hands, not enough to fully dry her gown but it would do. With the fabric still wrinkled and damp, she shimmied the layers of red velvet over her head and laced the front stays.

Finlay's tunic and vest lay bunched near the river and she picked up his discarded clothing, dried it as well as she could then folded and left his clothes with a small rock overtop to weight them down should the wind rise.

She splish-splashed across the muddy marsh oozing thick and heavy with the additional rainfall then at the edge of the woods, found her soggy slippers and slapped them on. Along the forest path, she trod.

As the sun rose over the horizon, it sent a stunning blaze of gold and red across the lightening sky and the formidable stone walls of Matheson House rose before her. She hurried through the gates and ducked into the lingering shadows of the curtain wall as a score of warriors strode out in their battle attire, their weapons holstered at their sides.

She crept inside, dashed up the side steps and walked into her chamber.

"Good morn, my lady." Effie rose from the hearth where she'd lit her fire and dusted her hands against her aproned sides. "I ordered a bath for you. What do you wish to wear?"

"The silvery-blue gown, please. Lay it on the bed if you could, and then ask Julia if she could join me. I need to speak to her." Two minds were always better than one, and right now, she needed her sister's advice on all that had occurred.

"Aye, my lady." Effie laid out the gown requested then tugged the tub from the corner into the area in front of the fire and left.

Two lanky lads with their shirttails fluttering loose over their tan breeches carried in pails of hot water and poured it into the tub while another maid added vanilla scented oil and a sprinkle of dried rose petals. Done, the maid closed the door behind her after the servants had filed out.

Longing to be done with her damp gown still chaffing her skin, she shed it and her sark then sank into the glorious water. 'Twas wonderful and warmed her through. She dunked her head and when she came back up, Julia stood inside her chamber, her golden locks coiled high on her head with two loose spiral curls bouncing free at each side.

"You asked for me, and I'm glad you did." Her sister crossed to her in a swish of her emerald skirts. "I was so worried when Finlay set out after you. Where have you been all night?"

"I ran to the cove and spent the night in the cavern with him. I have so much to tell you." She built up a lather with the bar of soap and scrubbed her hair with the mass of bubbles. "I exhausted my fire."

"What?" In a flurry of skirts, Julia knelt at the tub's edge. "But 'tis impossible. I've never heard of a fire-wielder doing so afore."

"Neither have I, but 'tis the truth. I couldnae even bring forth a flicker of heat until this morn. My fire still has yet to fully return." Hands raised, she wriggled her fingertips and two fingers caught alight. Her fire was reigniting. She dragged more of her heat from the well deep within her and lit another three fingers. The moment she did, the last five flared to life with ease.

"Well, it appears you now have your fire back."

"With no fire, there was no way I could harm Finlay." She slid under the water, rinsed her hair and popped back up with a grin.

"You joined as one?" Excitement shimmered in Julia's voice. "Tell me you did."

"We did. We also spoke handfast vows then completed the bond and created a merged link of the mind."

"But you are here now, and without him. Where is he?"

"After I awoke, I snuck out. He's still under Isla's compulsion and of course willnae remember me since we've parted ways. I must remedy all I've done, as soon as I can." She grasped her sister's hand where it rested on the rim. "The four elements came together last eve in a perfect storm. Fire came in the form of lightning, water in the form of rain, air in the form of the fierce wind that rose, and with the earth, we were deep inside the cavern when the storm unleashed itself."

"Incredible." Julia clutched a hand to her chest. "This is wonderful news, that your fire can be exhausted, and in that time it's gone allow a joining with your mate. I wonder if such a merging of the elements again will exhaust your fire."

"I have to hold onto the hope that it will. Surely it could no' have been just a one-time occurrence. Although I need to need to test that theory to know for sure, which means I'll need a mate who remembers me." She lit her fingers and blew on the tips until the flames lengthened. With only one thought, she snuffed them back out. "The one thing I certainly learnt last eve was that I cannae continue to hide from him, no' now we've created the merged link of the mind."

"Then we need to speak to Isla. She will be ecstatic to hear of the storm and that you completed the bond. If you exhausted your fire once, then there is hope you'll be able to do so again. Allow me to fix your hair afore we leave. It's been knotted into an awful mess by whatever you've gotten up to." Giggling, Julia gently detangled her hair. She separated it into sections then ran the comb through it before drying it with a cloth. "All done."

"Aye, finding Isla is imperative." She hopped out of the water and dried herself. Quickly, she donned a clean sark from her trunk, picked up the silvery-blue gown the maid had left and eased it over her head. The soft satin folds shimmered over her hips and swished to her ankles.

"I am so excited for you." Julia shuffled in behind her and laced her stays with jittery fingers. "You are each other's match in every way. 'Tis wonderful to know that is the case."

"You dinnae believe I hope too highly? What if I'm wrong about the storm and the combining of the elements? What if my fire never extinguishes itself again even when another perfect storm strikes?"

"You are soul bound, and there is no hope greater than that of the mated bond. I have faith you will find a way to extinguish your fire again since you've already done so." She turned her by the shoulders and pinched her cheeks. "Which means you must. Now, 'tis time to live your life to the fullest, no matter where that journey might take you. Let's be away."

"Thank you, Julia. I love you." Her heart full, she slid her matching slippers on and followed her sister out the door. They walked down the winding stairs and entered the great hall abuzz with warriors attired in their clan plaids. Kenneth sat at the dais, although Gilleoin, Aunt Sorcha and Nessa still remained at the village and would until they'd convinced the leaders of the need for all within the village to seek refuge during the coming battle, one that would rise in mere days. June the eleventh approached with speed.

"Do you see Isla?" Hand to her brow, Julia peered about on the tips of her toes. Warriors sat at trestle tables with steaming bowls of oats and fresh loaves of bread before them. They ate with gusto and much chatter and din. "Oh, there she is. At the front door."

Isla, her hand resting within the bend of Iain's elbow, walked outside with her mate, Kirk right behind them. Both Finlay's brothers were dressed in black leather pants and dark tunics under padded cotuns, their claymores glinting at their sides. With the coming battle looming, all had to be prepared for the MacKenzie's strike and they appeared ready for training.

"We'll catch them up." Julia grasped her hand and tugged her along after her.

Outside in the bailey, the warriors trained in their kilts, dust pluming at their feet and steel ringing loud as they struck each other. A tall burly warrior stomped to the center of the group in thick fur boots with a gong in hand. He called for the change and several warriors swapped out with men on the sidelines before the battling once again resumed.

Iain halted at the center well draped in ivy, kissed Isla's cheek then strode with Kirk to the training area. The two warmed up, twirling their blades in a precise figure eight. Then they tapped their swords together and fought, swiftly and with immense strength.

"Isla!" Julia waved out and they both hurried across and joined her at the well.

"Good morning to you two." Isla hugged Julia and her, a welcoming smile on her face.

"We have much to speak to you about." In a flurry, Arabel recited all that happened between her and Finlay while Isla listened with wide eyes and a rising smile.

"That is the best news." The wind lifted, fluttered Isla's sapphire skirts and the white ribbon at the top of her cinched bodice. "What you've told me also explains why Iain sensed a great deal of contentment coming from Finlay last night, ecstatic contentment. Kirk got a blast of it too, and I sat quietly with hope in my heart that things might have changed for you both. It does sound as if the realignment of the elements occurred during the storm, and I love that it extinguished your fire. There's hope, always hope to keep us strong."

"Aye, but I left without waking Finlay this morn, and there willnae be a chance he'll remember me, or our joining."

"I agree, and unfortunately I can't reverse what I've compelled. All his memories of his time with you are gone. I also can't tamper with his thought processes and try to reinstall them, or else he'll begin to believe he's gone mad. There is a fine line to what I can and can't do." Isla's gaze softened. "He's your mate, Arabel, and I can never compel that truth from him, that is why, deep in his heart, he completed the bond with you the first moment he could. Doing so rages through our shifter men, their desire to tie their chosen one to them all that rides them. Did you successfully create the merged link of the mind?"

"We did, and if you are in agreement, I would like you to remove the compulsion from Finlay and his brothers, provided Finlay too desires it."

"He might be angry at the lengths we took to keep you from him, but he'll never turn you away. You're not alone, and never will be. You have an entire clan, your sister and me, and the 'power of three' on your side. There is no limit to what we'll be able do to help you find all the answers you seek." She glanced toward the gates and raised a brow. "Oh, and it appears the time for some of those answers has now arrived."

Fury lined Finlay's brow as he marched toward his brothers, his wrinkled white tunic un-tucked and flapping over his tan rawhide pants, his brown leather vest slung over one shoulder. The stubble razzing his jaw was thick and dark, his black hair a wind-tossed mess and a mass of emotions swirling within the golden depths of his eyes. He tossed his vest to the ground and heaved his sword from its side scabbard, his rage evident as he slammed his blade into Iain's.

She should never have denied her mate. The time for her reckoning had arrived.

* * * *

So many intense and fierce emotions barreled through Finlay. He'd awoken in a cavern on a ledge overhanging a cool freshwater pool some miles from the castle, all alone and with only slivers of memory to mark the time. He'd been chasing a woman with long blond locks that swayed to her waist and vivid red skirts. She was nameless, faceless, yet everything about her called to him, on the deepest level. She was also the same unknown woman who'd haunted his dreams over the past few days. He ached, so deep in his soul he could barely breathe through the pain, and his heart, it felt as if it had been torn in two, as if he'd never be whole again.

"Whoa." Iain backed up a step. "What's going on?"

"I need help." He swung again, striking Iain's blade hard and fast a second time. "I can't bear the weight of this loss thundering through me a moment more. I can't find her."

"You mean your mate?" Kirk jumped in and met Finlay's next strike. "Yet I sensed only contentment coming from you last night, and an overwhelming amount of it."

"If I was content, that emotion has well and truly gone. This morning I awoke inside a cavern deep within the cliffs at the cove, and I have no idea why I did. There was also no sign of anyone but me, yet I'm certain I was with someone. I'm running out of time and she needs me, just as badly as I need her."

"Finlay, I'm so sorry."

He stumbled to his knees, grasped his head.

"Are you all right?" Iain fell to one knee beside him, Kirk dropping down on his other side.

He searched his mind, found the pathway those sweet words had been delivered along. "I don't believe it," he whispered to his brothers. "There's a telepathic link between me and another."

"You've completed the bond?" Wild confusion lit Iain's face, likely the same wild confusion racing across his own. "How could you not remember joining with your mate?"

"C-come to the chief's solar, Finlay." Her voice flowed through, all shaky and pained. *"I-I promise to explain everything where we'll be afforded more privacy."*

"Who are you?" He found his footing and stood. "Chief's solar," he said to Iain and Kirk and took off, his brothers hot on his heels. He pounded into the great hall, skidded around the corner and flew into the side antechamber bereft of its chief but instead holding Isla and Julia standing either side of Julia's sister who sat in a padded chair. He strode toward her. "Arabel, isn't it? You're the fire-wielder? Is it you who just spoke to me?"

"Aye, I did." She bunched her hands in her lap and twisted her fingers within the silvery-blue folds of her skirts.

"How"—he seized the arms of her wooden chair and scraped

it closer, bringing them nose to nose—"did you manage to do that?"

"Finlay, calm down." Kirk shut the door, pulled out a chair and plunked it behind him. Kirk gripped his shoulders and urged him down. "No looming over the poor lass."

Iain eyed Isla and the two clearly spoke, although along their merged link and by the look on Iain's face, he wasn't happy with whatever he'd just discovered.

Scrubbing a hand over his heavily whiskered jaw, Finlay faced the women he'd created a merged link with. Arabel trembled, her head bowed and her gaze on her whitened knuckles. Aye, he needed to take more care. She was scared and he'd caused her to be so.

Slowly, he leaned forward and covered one of her hands with his. She was cold, and for one who wielded fire, she shouldn't be. That he knew to the depths of his soul. He pulled back an inch, lost the contact he needed but assuaged the fear taking hold of him instead. "What is going on?"

"I've done you a grave wrong." She lifted her gaze and those beautiful eyes of hers glimmered with tears. One trickled free, trailed down her soft cheek and splashed her gown.

He touched the salty drop with one finger and shook his head. Hell, he'd made his mate cry and that was the last thing he wanted to do. "Please, don't cry."

"I'm so sorry. This is all my fault." More tears, and as each one fell, they hit him like he'd taken a spear to his gut. "When emotions of grief or loss rise, so too does my cold-fire. It makes me cold."

"Then fix your cold-fire, right now." Her talk of it set him completely on edge, although he knew not why. "Hurry."

"Of course." She closed her eyes and remained quiet. Long minutes passed before her cheeks finally flushed and she ceased trembling. When she lifted her lashes, she looked into his eyes and he almost drowned within the watery blue depths lit by sparks of gold around the edges.

"Are you feeling better?"

"A little." She gulped. "Finlay, when you first discovered we were mated, you were so determined to complete the bond even though doing so would have ended in your death. In the past two centuries only six fire-wielders have been born afore me with the skill of fire and all have perished following the death of their loved one. There is no intimacy permitted with one who wields fire."

"Yet we've clearly been intimate and I survived such a joining. What happened at the cove?"

"Yesterday, I ran there and you chased me. You wouldnae give up the fight and when the storm hit, we took shelter in the cavern. Fire came in the form of lightning, water in the form of rain, air in the form of the fierce wind that rose, and the earth, well we were deep inside the cavern when the storm unleashed itself. My fire was exhausted and I couldnae raise even a glimmer of heat. The four elements had come back into realignment."

"Fire, water, air and earth." He mumbled the words, although they roared inside his mind, as if he'd spoken them many times before. "Has your fire been out of control since our arrival in this time?" The knowledge flittered at the edges of his mind, wispy and frail but still there.

"That's right. During the storm we completed the bond, when we knew 'twas safe to do so." She lit her fingers and flames danced on her fingertips. "Now the realignment has occurred, I no longer release heat for no reason, but I shall always be susceptible to losing control during moments of intimacy. That I can never control."

"I see." He reached for her hands and she doused her fire and threaded her fingers through his.

"You've told me many times that we are each other's match, that we wouldnae have been mated otherwise. I believe, but in reaching this point, I took many precautions. To ensure your safety, I asked Isla to compel you and your brothers. She wouldn't to begin with, no' until I forced your hand and you too asked her to do so. I was to be no one to you, no more than another woman who resided here within this keep. No one of interest or importance. No one to draw too much of your curiosity. And should we have met, each instance would have been as if the first and all other times forgotten."

"Well, that explains a damn lot. No wonder I can't remember you, except you took a grave risk by your actions. Those who are mated work best together, not apart as you've forced us to be." Frustration had reared and wouldn't abate. She'd chosen to leave him, when mated pairs never did.

"There is more." She slid her fingers from his and eased his shirt collar to one side. "You and your brothers cannae see it, but there is a mark here, one I placed on you a few days ago, a mark I—well, I bit you again during our joining."

"You had all three of us compelled?" She'd gone to dire lengths. He swept her silky blond hair back from her neck and exposed two marks, one on each side of her neck, both gracing her creamy flesh. His marks. His claim. On his woman. Only he never remembered giving them to her. "I can see your marks."

"You bit me last eve for the first time. You had no' done so afore." She cleared her throat, her cheeks flushing an even rosier hue.

"I want my memories back, to know everything that's transpired between us." He looked deep into her eyes and his pulse raced. She was the one who'd stolen his heart, and the one without question, who he'd hand it back to again and again. "And I mean desperately."

"Isla cannae return lost memories, only remove her compelling command and ensure you dinnae lose any more." She settled back in her chair, creating a distance—albeit a small one— he didn't care for, not one little bit. "'Tis up to you though if you wish for her to do so. I forced your agreement the first time, and I shall no' do so again."

"Of course I wish the compelling command gone." His mate clearly liked to take matters into her own hands, but he wouldn't allow it a moment longer. Suspicion though shimmered through him. "Why wouldn't I wish it?"

Arabel glanced at Isla and his brother's mate dragged in a deep breath and stepped forward. "I'm aware of what's been recorded in history, and the very last known fire-wielder to have ever lived, passed away during the battle at the village on June the eleventh. Which means you could still very well lose Arabel on that day, whether you wish it or not."

Isla's words sent a shockwave of cold blazing through his veins. There wasn't a chance he'd lose his mate, not now he'd finally found her. He'd ensure her safety, keep her right here at the castle where she'd remain well away from any harm. No one was taking his mate from him again, not his woman with her decision to keep his memories from him, or a looming battle he and his brothers intended to change the outcome of. "Remove your compelling command, Isla." He kept his gaze on Arabel. "I won't forget my woman, not one more time."

"Of course." Isla began, her sweetly hypnotic words flowing over him. "Finlay, Iain, and Kirk, you'll remain perfectly still and listen to me well. Finlay is mated to Arabel and all three of you are aware of it. You shall never forget this conversation we've had or her again. She is important to all of us. So too, the mark upon Finlay's neck shall once again be seen. Do you hear and understand me?"

"Aye," he and his brothers said.

"Good." She clapped and he blinked the daze away. "Finlay, you may kiss your handfast wife."

"What? My handfast wife?"

"Oh dear." Arabel clasped a hand to her mouth.

"Hell, Arabel. What else have you forgotten to tell me?" He grasped her hips and lifted her onto his lap and mind to mind, whispered, *"No more secrets, because there is no limit to what I'll do to claim you.*"

"*So I've learnt.*" She wrapped her arms around his neck. "*You're my warrior, my lover, the other half of my soul. I love you, Finlay.*"

Her declaration shimmered through his mind, and his heart swelled as he tucked her words safely away inside him, just as he tucked her even closer against him. "*Why do I feel as if you've said that to me before?*"

"*Because I have.*"

She wasn't just his mate, not now. She was his entire heart, his only reason for living, the only person he could never survive without. "*There is none who I will ever love as greatly as I love you. My wife, my lover, and the other half of my soul.*"

"*You spoke those words to me after we completed the bond. You were wonderful by the way. Making love with you was magical, and far beyond my wildest dreams.*"

"*Woman, you are about to get yourself tossed over my shoulder and taken back to that cave.*"

"*You tasted delicious too.*" A brighter blush burst across her cheeks. "*I wish to taste you again if it is ever possible.*" She giggled, and the sweet sound brought him such joy.

"*We'll make sure it's possible.*" He stood, did exactly as he'd warned and tossed her over his shoulder. He needed time alone with her. Just them and no other. He needed her, even more than he needed his next breath.

Chapter 10

Arabel gasped as Finlay slung her over his shoulder and her belly thumped into his rock hard shoulder. He bounded from the chief's solar, through the great hall and upstairs.

"Your chamber. Which floor?" he demanded as he raced with her.

"The third, the last door on the left." Her blond hair dangled down over his firm backside and with one hand on each of his cheeks, she stroked his tight butt in slow circles. As no lady should do, but she couldn't help herself. "I'm almost certain there's a better way to carry me than this."

"Not when I need one hand free to fend off anyone in case you squeal." He patted her rear. "We also need to talk about last night and all that transpired, preferably without any interruptions."

"Then I shall definitely be squealing, but for an entirely different reason."

"So you agree we need some time alone?"

"I do."

"Good." He kept one hand firm around the back of her knees as he marched down the corridor lit by a hazy beam of sunshine streaming through the narrow window at the end of the hallway. At the last chamber on the left, he opened the thickly paneled door and bolted it shut behind him. "Is this your room alone?"

"Aye, and you've been here afore. The night we first met at the loch in the woods, Julia asked you to watch over me since my fire had flared so badly, and after I'd cooled down, you returned with me and insisted on remaining in my chamber. You decreed we were mated, and you wouldnae leave." She gripped his back and eased herself up enough to loop her arms around his neck. The move made him lose his over-the-shoulder hold and she slid down his chest and into his arms. "You settled yourself in the corner chair to sleep, although that lasted all of a few minutes. You slept in my bed for what remained of the night."

"Did anything transpire between us?"

"We talked, and by the morn I too sensed what you did and could no longer refute we were mated. We kissed and I marked you."

"And did I attempt to mark you in return?" His sinfully sexy eyes glimmered.

"You asked for my permission, but I wouldnae allow it, or I should say my loss of control wouldnae allow it. My heat rose and you had to toss cold water on me to cool me down."

"Interesting." He carried her to the bed and laid her across the soft brown fur covering her mattress. Gently, he nudged her knees apart and with his legs between hers, sank down on top of her. "I would like another kiss."

She wriggled underneath him, her breath catching. "This is the exact place where we kissed the first time, and right afore we did, you spoke of your feelings."

"Repeat what I said. I want to hear it, word for word." A sensual spark of heat lit his golden eyes.

"I will never desire any other than you." She touched his lower lip with one finger and embraced the warmth of his body overtop of hers. "That's what you said."

"That is exactly how I feel in this moment." He licked his lip, his tongue sweeping across her finger. "Nothing has changed.

Losing you is something I'll never survive, not now I've finally found you. The thought I've lost so many memories of our time together though pains me."

"I'm sorry. You told me afore that losing me is something you'd never survive and now I believe you." She slid her fingers into his silky black hair and stroked his scalp. "After we kissed, you told me you wanted the right to sleep in my bed each and every night."

"Aye, your bed is now my bed, my wife." He touched his mouth to hers, his lips so achingly soft as he joined them together. Gently, playfully, he kissed her, licking her tongue and sucking her lower lip into his mouth. Desire swarmed her senses and her breasts swelled under his chest, her hard nipples scraping the silk of her gown. Deep need and raw sensation speared through her. Then he rubbed his body against hers, until his scent surrounded her and hers enveloped him.

"I cannae believe we're kissing, that I can finally speak to you of all that's happened between us."

"I may not have my memories, but the emotions have remained. Holding you again, is like having the other half of my soul returned." His breath whispered softly across her lips in a teasing caress she hungered for more of.

"Kiss me again, please. I need more."

"Always." He groaned, deep and throaty before capturing her mouth and offering her exactly what she'd asked for. His kiss, so sweetly seductive had her gasping for breath.

"We must still take care. I will lose control if there is too much intimacy."

"I want to bite you, Arabel, to mark you and know I'll retain this memory."

"Aye, I need that too." She swept her hair away from the side of her neck and offered herself up to him. "Should my heat flare, there is a pail of water under my side table."

"I'll be careful."

"I know you will. I have faith and hope now as never afore." She wrapped her legs around his hips and sighed with delight as his cock lengthened and poked into her belly. "I'm sorry we cannae join fully together as we did in the cavern. I cannae allow that deep of an intimacy when 'twill be too much for me to bear. My skill will rise without question should we take things too far."

"We'll test the whole combining of elements again and find a way to be together. I won't rest until we've discovered a solution." He nuzzled her neck, licked her skin and sucked it deep inside his mouth. "May I touch you wherever I please?"

Arching into his divine touch, she murmured, "Aye. I am yours to touch as you wish."

"Well, I really like this subservient side of you, in case I haven't told you so before." He slid one hand inside her bodice and palmed her breast. He caressed her flesh then bit down and marked her. A fierce rumble vibrated against her skin, his bear so close to the surface, and an exquisite heat washed through her, pulsed down to her core and made her thoughts tumble into disarray.

"Once more," he breathed as he brushed her hair clear of the other side of her neck. His mouth descended and she cupped the back of his head, held him against her and gasped as he marked her again.

"Oh goodness, so good." Heat shimmered from her and rippled her red bed curtains. She focused, found her inner strength and held firm. "I cannae take any more intimacy, other than that."

"Got it. Your limit after a little kissing is two bites. Although you need to get ready for a little nudity. My bear wishes to meet you since he too lost his memories as I did." He lifted himself from her, his delicious weight gone from one breath to the next. Then he stood over her and shucked his tunic. His chest, so broad and heavily muscled, made her fingers itch to touch him.

"The first night we met, we swam together and you shifted in front of me. I like your bear." She sat up. "I got to pet him."

"He's demanding to meet you, and he can't wait any longer." He unstrapped his sword belt, propped his weapon and daggers against the side table, kicked off his black boots and shoved his rawhide pants down his legs and off. Then he stepped back and made the Change in one swift and sizzling display. As the bright lights dispersed, his bear plodded toward her. He slapped his paws down on the bed either side of her and nudged her hands with his muzzle.

Transfixed, she looked into his golden eyes and sank her hands into his pelt and scratched between his ears. Black fur, so silky and soft, tickled her fingertips.

"Finlay?" Leaning forward, she brushed a kiss across his forehead.

"I'm here, my sweet."

"Does it hurt to shift?"

"The Change is swift and any pain sears through for only a miniscule moment. It's gone as quickly as it comes." He made the Change again, fur retracting and muzzle shortening in a shimmer of bright lights until her man stood naked before her.

"'Tis best you dress and remove any temptation from my sight. You've more clothes in your traveling sack which is by my trunk." She motioned toward the bag he'd placed in her chamber that first night. "You left it here."

"I wondered where that had gotten to. I had to borrow more clothes from Kenneth." He nabbed the bag and set it on the end of her bed, released the leather strap on the top and foraged inside. He donned a clean pair of black leather pants and a dark blue tunic with detailed embroidery along the collar, a tunic she'd made for Kenneth for his last birthday.

Smiling, she straightened his collar and on her toes, pressed her lips to the mark she'd given him last night, right where his neck and shoulder met. One lick and nip settled her deep inside, or at least for the moment. "Your bear is beautiful, if one can call a bear so."

"He's calmed down, and with only one pat and a kiss on the forehead from you, but right now I'll need to keep my hands busy to keep from reaching for you." At the side table, he strapped on his sword belt and dagger then poured water from the jug into the basin and lathered the soap.

Outside, a thick layer of gray cloud swept across the sky and she gripped the stone windowsill. The wind breezing through the open window whipped her blond hair about her face and plastered her silk bodice to her chest. The sea swelled and white-capped waves rolled into shore. "Another storm is brewing."

"Hell, I hope so." Grinning, he smeared bubbles across his jaw. "You've explained that you ran from me yesterday and I chased you to the cove, but what happened during the time between then and when Isla first compelled me."

"Three days passed during that time and I assuaged my need for you by watching you train. I missed you terribly, to the point where I was bathing in the pool three times a day just to settle my flaring heat. Never have I lost control as I have since your arrival, and glad I am the elements have realigned."

"I barely got any sleep during those days, not when a nameless, faceless woman kept tormenting me in my dreams." He smeared bubbles over his jaw then angled the looking glass to the right position. From the sheath on the inside of his wrist, he slid his dagger free and ran the blade from his ear to his chin. "There were also fleeting images of a pool of water rippling under a moonlit sky, and I knew something had happened there, something important, but I just couldn't hold onto the memory. Then when I awoke in the cavern, it was from a dream where I'd been chasing a lass with long blond locks and vivid red skirts. Everything about you called to me, even though I'd been compelled to forget you. You tore my heart in two with your leaving. I ached, so deep in my soul I could barely breathe through the pain."

"I'm so sorry." She crossed to him, unable to handle the

distance between them, even though only a few short feet. "So sorry."

"I didn't tell you to upset you, but so you understood how deep my feelings for you ran even under compulsion, how deep they will always run." He propped his butt on the side table then held out his blade for her to take. "Although you could make it all up to me. I'm terrible at shaving myself, always nicking my skin."

"In the future, you use an electric shaver." She accepted the blade, eager to have all forgiven and forgotten between them. "You told me they're a device which plugs into a power source called electricity, and when that is turned on, the shaver has sharp metal rotating heads that slice the stubble off at the root. No soap and blade is necessary."

"That's right. When did I speak of electric shavers?" Hands on her waist, fingers warm and wide, he tugged her into the gap made in the V of his spread legs.

"When I shaved you the first time, the morning after you shared my bed, right here in this very spot." She tapped his jaw shut and shaved the bristles around his lips, swiftly and precisely, until his skin was smooth. Gently, she dabbed his skin dry with the cloth and kissed his chin. "There, all done."

"I think not. You missed my mouth by an inch." He took the dagger from her and sheathed it. "I need to kiss you, and you appear to have cooled sufficiently."

"Most sufficiently, and I crave your—" He covered her mouth with his and claimed his kiss, a delicious and sensual twining of their tongues and breath. "More," she whispered against his lips.

A chilling horn shrilled outside with one long and eerie blast. Finlay broke their kiss and bounded to the window and wedged sideways out to get a better look.

"That's the alert from the point watchman." She snuck in under his arm. Out in the bay, fishermen pulled in their nets as the skies grew darker and the waves rolled in heavier and higher.

"One blast means an unknown vessel approaches the castle, and a second sounds if an attack is imminent."

"We've still another two days until the MacKenzie burns the village to the ground. June the eleventh, at the stroke of midnight. That is the day and the hour he comes."

"There's been no second—"

The horn trumpeted again and a chill raced down her spine. "My grandmother would have warned us. Very little passes her by."

"Maybe there wasn't time. Our arrival in the past has already caused a change in events with our mated bond taking form. Anything is possible." He gripped her arms, his gaze intent. "You're to stay here within the safety of this castle. Find Isla and remain with her. She too isn't allowed to go anywhere near the battlefield. I won't lose you."

"You need only worry about yourself, because if you get hurt, even one scratch, I willnae be happy."

"I'll be careful. I promise you that." He swiped his black padded cotun from his bag and flew out the door, his voice whispering through her mind, "*You are the reason my heart beats. Be here when I return.*"

* * * *

Finlay didn't care to be parted from Arabel, not so soon after they'd been reunited, but he and his brothers had traveled through time for this very reason, to save the fae village and their future line from extinction, to give hope to their people, both in the future and in the past.

He wouldn't fail Arabel, her kin or his.

Taking the steps two at a time, he raced downstairs and whisked outside into the swirling rush of wind. A mass of black cloud whirled and seethed overhead. Ahead, Iain and Kirk ran through the front gate and he chased after them and caught them up at the stables. "What have you heard?" he yelled to Iain over the gale.

"A guardsman has confirmed two galleys are sailing toward us and on course for the village." Iain grasped his shoulder. "We'll need to ride there with all speed. The battle is about to begin."

Kirk hauled on a black war coat then slid a second sword into a baldric across his back and tossed Finlay a bow and satchel of arrows. Finlay slung it across his shoulders as shouts boomed all around and more men swarmed into the area. A good twenty warriors mounted their horses while an equal number raced down the trail to the sea-gate. Out at sea, two galleys with their massive square sails caught the strong wind and barreled toward the village. Their bows rose in the heavy swell and dumped down hard. So many lives to save. He wouldn't fail Arabel's people.

Kenneth, Gilleoin's eldest son, raced out the front gate as lightning speared the skies. He sprinted down to the stone landing and leapt onto one of the waiting birlinns. "All to oars," he bellowed as he gripped the center mast. "There can be no delay. We'll head the MacKenzies off."

"Let's go." Iain bounded onto a war horse, as did Kirk.

Finlay snagged a destrier from its tethered post, mounted and knees thrust into the animal's flanks, slapped the reins against its neck and tore along the trail leading along the curve of the bay. They rode with a score of warriors, leaving a plume of dust the rushing wind whipped around in their wake.

He urged his mount faster along the narrow path that wound upward along the ocean's cliff-top. Massive pine trees swayed on his left and branches grazed his arm, while on his right, the sea roared and his horse scattered stones on the verge that clacked down the rock face before disappearing into the churning, watery depths below.

The two MacKenzie galleys approached fast, and Kenneth sailed directly toward them. It was so close, no telling yet who would win the race to the village first, Kenneth or the MacKenzies.

"We have to hurry," he bellowed to his brothers over the fury of the storm. He rode hard, as they all did, desperate to the reach the village in time.

* * * *

"Julia!" Arabel raced into her sister's chamber but found Isla instead gripping the windowsill with white knuckles as she peered out over the inner courtyard and the loch beyond.

"She's not here and this battle has arrived two days too soon." Isla rushed across to her, her golden shifter gaze swirling with turmoil. "I can't shift while I'm expecting and I can't compel when I'm not where I need to be. Iain demanded I wait with you and Julia, but the villagers are my people just as much as those in this castle are."

"Finlay asked me to find you, to remain with you." Fear sent cold-fire racing through her and she called forth her skill and directed a blast of hot fire to warm her through. Too much, too fast. It singed her and she clutched her chest and fell to her knees.

"Arabel?" Isla dropped down beside her.

"I'll be fine." Gasping for breath, she thrust up a hand. "Just dinnae touch me."

"Where are you hurt?"

"Too much hot fire. I should have taken more care." One thoughtless loss of control could kill her. Shakily, she shoved to her feet, at least grateful her fast action had warmed her through. "I'll recover."

"My lady." Effie rushed into the room in her white aproned skirts. "Lady Julia left the chief's solar no' long after you and told me she wished to visit your parents' memorial stone afore she no longer could."

"My parents' stone lies at the edge of the village." She raced for the door. "Isla, I have to go. I cannae leave my sister out there with the battle about to rage."

"Then I'm coming with you." She hurried after her. "I should never have allowed Iain to leave without me. The 'power of three' shouldn't go into battle without their chosen ones at their sides, and that includes both you and me. Now we need to make sure no harm comes to any of them. I'll watch over one and all."

"As I'll do the same." She had one of the strongest of the battle skills and she intended to use it. Her place was at Finlay's side, whether he wished it or not.

Chapter 11

The horn trumpeted across the bay from the direction of the castle, not once but twice. Nessa froze on the pebbly beach next to Julia who'd arrived mere minutes ago on horseback along the cliff-top forest trail. As a seer, she should have had another vision when her people's very lives were at stake. She hadn't, and what it meant, she had no idea.

"The enemy approaches." Nessa wrapped one arm around Julia's waist as out at sea, two MacKenzie galleys cruised toward them. A Matheson birlinn sailed in a direct line to cut them off, Kenneth at the helm.

Kenneth shouted over the crashing of the waves as he gripped the ropes and strained to control the wind power he'd harnessed in the vessel's tight sail. "Hold tight," he barked to his men. The bow rose sharply upward then slammed back down, and their enemy whizzed by in front of them.

Beside her, Gilleoin bellowed orders to a score of his warriors who'd assembled on the foreshore, while another score of men rode free of the forest trail edging the cliffs and galloped down to the beach.

Iain, Finlay, and Kirk, bounded from their mounts and raced toward them.

Finlay skidded in beside Julia. "I've left Arabel at the castle with Isla and you need to return to her, now. Your sister will never survive this battle if anything happens to you."

"She'll never survive if aught happens to you either." Julia hugged him. "Please be careful. I'll seek shelter in the woods. 'Tis too late for me to return to the castle."

Thunder boomed and an arrow thunked into the ground at their feet, right between Finlay and his brothers. Finlay hauled his bow from over his shoulder, planted his feet wide and set an arrow into the notch. He eyed his target and released his shot. The arrow flew in a wide arc and slammed into the leg of the archer standing at the bow of the MacKenzie galley. The man toppled over the side and Finlay slid another arrow into place. "Nessa, get Julia far away from here. Hurry."

"Aye, I shall." She grabbed Julia's hand and ran toward Sorcha as she waited at the edge of the forest. She left the three warriors standing strong side by side. There was naught more she could now do. 'Twas now time to allow the 'power of three' to rise.

Chapter 12

Matheson Castle, Scotland, current day.

In his solar, Murdock Matheson fell to his knees under the weight of a powerful vision. The battle had begun, although two days too soon. What the hell had brought it on earlier?

Armed and prepared for war, the 'power of three' stood together on the beach amongst Gilleoin's men as two galleys filled to the brim with MacKenzies careened across the massive swell toward them. Another birlinn teeming with Matheson warriors missed the next cresting wave. They were too far behind. The MacKenzies would outnumber those on shore two to one.

"All to arms." Gilleoin shoved his sword-arm high into the air and bellowed as forty or more warriors stood primed and ready at his back. "We fight, for freedom and for our very survival. Let us take these blackguards down."

The MacKenzie galleys landed on the beach and their warriors exploded from their vessels and bounded onto shore, shouting their victorious arrival. Then they swarmed forward into the waiting Mathesons and swords clashed.

Murdock's vision wavered, then another array of images flared to life. Isla and Arabel galloped along the forest path, the sea roaring and slamming into the rock wall a hundred feet below while a fierce wind whipped around and lightning slashed the skies.

Tension coiled deep within him and had nowhere to go. His kin were about to battle for their very lives and all he could do was watch and wait.

Chapter 13

Alongside his brothers, Finlay hauled his claymore from his scabbard. Together, they released a bloodcurdling battle cry and rushed forward into the fray of fierce MacKenzies.

A warrior came at Finlay and he blocked the swift blow, their claymores clashing dead center, steel clanging loud against steel. "Stay close," he yelled to Iain and Kirk. "We're strongest when we fight side by side."

"I'm right beside you." On his right, Iain slashed his blade against his adversary's. "We need to hold them back until Kenneth gets here and we even these odds up a bit."

Kirk grunted and met two attackers head on, striking first one and then the other. "We can't let even one of them pass us by. They're not to get to the village."

"I agree." With his brothers at his side, Finlay fought. Sweat poured from his body while high above a tumultuous mass of dark, seething clouds blackened the sky and promised a storm unlike any other, a storm that raged right here on the land in equal measure.

"*Finlay?*" Arabel's worried voice washed through his mind, her tone filled with panic and fear.

"*I'm here.*" He struck his opponent hard and his hit brought the MacKenzie warrior to his knees. He knocked him out with the hilt of his sword then met his next attacker who jumped over his comrade. He slashed, attacked, fast and hard.

"Behind you," she screamed. *"A MacKenzie has snuck around."*

He spun about, and his enemy struck his ribs with his blade. Pain ricocheted through him and he staggered back from the brutal sword blow. Damn bloodthirsty MacKenzies. They fought dirty, not meeting a man head on. Breath ragged, he shoved to his feet and gripped his side. No blood, but his cotun had been sliced open. A lucky break. "Keep your eyes on both sides," he shouted to his brothers then sprang forward and fought.

Weapons clashed then he ducked the MacKenzie's next high strike, rammed into him with one shoulder and took him down to the ground. The man hit his head on a rock and knocked himself out.

"I said you were no' allowed to come to any harm, Finlay."

"How did you know a warrior had snuck—damn it. Where are you?" He searched the cliff-side trail and found her. Arabel sat atop a horse next to Isla, the forest rising high behind them. *"You should never have come."*

"I'm your mate and where you go, I shall go. Kenneth comes. Keep your eyes on the fight until he does."

Beyond the breakers, their Matheson warriors plunged their oars into the sea and powered their vessel in. Kenneth pumped his fist into the air and ordered his men to lower the sail. They crested a large wave, cruised in and rushed ashore and into the melee.

"Stay where you're safe, Arabel. I won't lose you."

"As I won't lose you."

Another MacKenzie came at him and he shoved his blade high and met the fierce blow. He and his opponent matched each other in height and breadth, although that was no equal standing for the battle lust storming through his body. This was Matheson land, and the MacKenzies wouldn't be allowed to take the villagers' lives. He struck, landing several hard blows, one after the other then with one powerful strike of his claymore, knocked the man's sword away.

The warrior grabbed his dirk, his aim on course for between Finlay's eyes.

He ducked the dagger as it flew, kicked the warrior's feet out from under him then jumped back as fire rippled across the grass and licked at the MacKenzie warrior's clothing. The man bellowed and ran into the waves.

"Arabel, I said to stay where you're safe."

"I'm your mate and I will fight at your side." She rushed toward him, fire flaring from her fingertips and her blond hair streaming back from the raging winds circling them. She struck the MacKenzie battling Iain and the two fighting Kirk. All three of their enemy swatted the fire licking at their legs and sprinted into the water, just as his attacker had done.

Well, it appeared he'd underestimated his woman. She wielded one of the fiercest of the battle skills and he shouldn't have forgotten that. Still, he stepped in front of her and shielded her from any coming attacker. There wasn't a chance he'd lose her.

"Step aside for a moment." She ducked out from behind him and sent another arc of fire at another MacKenzie.

"Isla, get back!" Iain bellowed as he eyed Isla atop her horse.

"You need me," she yelled and rode along the warring front, her compelling voice strong. "All will cease fighting and listen to me well and true! Those warriors here from the MacKenzie clan will drop your weapons."

Their enemy's swords clattered to the ground, so swiftly Finlay gaped. Their women were strong.

"I'll be back as soon as I've contained my mate. She's impossible sometimes." Iain slapped Finlay's back then raced toward Isla and bounded onto the back of her mount and swept the reins from her. He half bent over her, protecting her as best as he could should anything fly toward her.

Still, Isla wouldn't be halted. Her compelling voice rang loud and clear even with Iain's looming. "Hear me well, MacKenzies. You'll gather your fallen and leave these shores. Your fight is done this day and you've lost the battle. Board your vessels and don't look back."

The MacKenzie warriors heaved their fallen comrades over their shoulders and stumbled toward their galleys.

"We were wrong to keep them away." Kirk sheathed his sword.

"Go," Isla commanded the MacKenzies. "Flee, as fast as you can, and know that the Mathesons are the 'Son of the Bear.' No one will take what is ours."

The MacKenzies boarded and with their oars in hand, rowed into the deep then raised their sails.

Isla grinned and continued, her voice so sweetly hypnotic. "Those here fighting for Gilleoin or to protect the village will tend our own wounded before we celebrate our win. I too am part of the 'power of three,' and our enemy will never get past any of us." She waved at Arabel from under Iain's arm. "Isn't that right, sister?"

"Aye, none will ever get past us." Arabel raised her hands high and sent an arc of fire streaming toward the fleeing MacKenzies. It rippled across their stern and sent their enemy speeding away.

Gilleoin shoved his sword high. "To the 'power of three' and their chosen ones! May they forever stand at each other's sides."

Cheers abounded and Nessa, Sorcha and Julia raced out of the forest with the villagers spilling out behind them.

With their enemy a mere dot on the horizon, Finlay tossed Arabel over his shoulder and hiked it toward his destrier as lightning sizzled overhead. "You are in so much trouble, my sweet."

"Oh, I hope so." She giggled, actually giggled. His woman

clearly had no self-preservation. "And I hope you noticed the perfect storm, my stubborn bear."

"Which will be your saving grace, since right now we're headed for the cavern. Isla and my brothers clearly have this battle in hand, whereas mine with you has just begun."

"Well, I do love a good battle." She patted his backside. "Hurry it along."

* * * *

Standing before her mate at the rear of the cavern on the small curve of sandy beach, Arabel unlaced her gown. She wriggled the silvery-blue silk down over her shift and folded it on top of a boulder as thunder rumbled overhead. "You said we are each other's match in every way, and I'm ready to accept our bond, fully and completely."

"As am I." He stripped off his cotun and tunic, laid his weapons safely against the rock wall until he remained clothed in only his black leather pants. "Can you read my mind?"

She could, with ease. He longed for her, just as she longed for him.

"Test your fire, my love."

From deep within, she tried to call it forth but nothing rose. "There is naught. I'm underground and all four elements are in place."

"Then it wasn't just the elements coming together in a perfect storm that caused the realignment, but also the four elements together which will continue to dispatch your fire."

"Aye, thank heavens it is that way." Her dreams had been answered and her hope now soared to new levels. She could have a life with him, one where they could join as one whenever the four elements came together again.

"Then in between storms, I believe I shall go slightly insane." Finlay swept her into his arms and bounded with her clasped tight to his chest onto the boulder leading toward the ledge. He jumped from one to the next then strode along the ledge toward the crack in the rock wall where spray misted through.

Gently, he set her on her feet beside him and she swayed closer, grazing his chest with her hard nipples. Her mind fuzzed, became consumed with the need to mate and join as one.

"Unless," he murmured, "the four elements needn't just be a brewing storm. There is water misting over us, the wind which is usually a constant outside, and I could easily create a fire pit at the back of the cave and ensure it is lit if there's no lightning. The element of fire should be acceptable no matter what form it comes in."

"And we are already underground. Do you think that might truly work?"

"We'll try it out once the storm has passed, before we leave this cave." He stroked down her sides, his gaze moving over her chest where her damp shift clung to her skin and outlined her breasts. "In the future, if what I hope works, we could build an underground home not far from Ivanson Castle and ensure it holds a fireplace, a very large and comfortable shower to provide the water, and if there isn't enough wind churning outside, I'll erect a wind machine that can easily be turned on."

"That sounds divine. I believe I'm going to enjoy the conveniences of your future time."

"I'm going to ensure it, and right now, you're tempting me beyond my endurance." He bent, fastened his mouth over her nipple and sucked it into his mouth, cloth and all. She moaned at the sweet sensations that rippled through her.

"That feels wonderful." She gripped the leather tie at the waist of his pants and pulled it free and passed it to him. "This is for you, afore I lose my mind."

"What is—ahh." He nodded and grinned. "A handfast binding. Perfect." He slipped the tie from her fingers, clasped his right hand with her right and wrapped the thin strip of leather around both their wrists. "Arabel, with all my heart and all that I am, I wish to bind us together as husband and wife, and before a year and a day passes, I'll ensure we're wed proper before our clans." He looked deep into her eyes. "I have fallen in love with you each and every time we've been together. That I know to the depths of my soul, and right now, I can't live another day without you at my side."

"You are my mate, my match in every way. I long to speak vows with you, vows you'll now remember."

"Then I'll begin." He lowered to his knees, caught her hands and brought them to his lips and kissed her knuckles. "I, Finlay Michael Matheson, of Ivanson Castle, pledge my troth to Arabel, of the House of Clan Matheson. With this handfast, I take her as my wife for the next year and a day, and as my mate for all time." He tightened his grip on her hand. "You'll be mine, in every single way."

She sank to her knees, her fingers twined with his. "I, Arabel, of the House of Clan Matheson, pledge my troth to Finlay Michael Matheson. With this handfast, I take him as my husband for the next year and a day, and as my mate for all time." She stared at the leather bound around their wrists and smiled as she raised her gaze to his. "Now we seal the vows with a kiss. We did so the first time."

"Are you sure?" A teasing glint lit his golden eyes.

"Aye, very sure." She captured his mouth and kissed him, until his hard body wrapped around and stamped hers with a fierce heat she needed more of.

"Whatever you need from me, you'll speak it." He looked deep into her eyes. "I want to know what you like, or what you don't like. What you'd prefer for me to do, or not do."

"As you told me the first time. I want to experience everything you can offer, Finlay, to be with you in every way, our bodies joined as one."

"Then first, I need to remove your shift." He tugged the leather strip binding their wrists free then rose to his feet and drew her up. "Is that acceptable?"

"I'm no' sure what's taking you quite so long."

"Because I'm as nervous as hell, woman. I've never lain with a lass before while you're far more experienced in the act of lovemaking and have bedded me." Grinning, he shook his head. "Which could only make sense between the two of us."

"If I remember correctly, you removed your trews first and I got to fondle and take your shaft in my mouth."

"That would never have happened first"—he tapped her nose—"not when your pleasure must come before all else."

"Ah well, 'twas worth a try." A sneaky giggle escaped her.

"I can see I'll have to keep my eyes on you, which I can't wait to do." He crouched, grasped her hem and lifted the cotton. With the fabric at her knees, he slid his hands over her calves, along the curves of her outer thighs until he exposed the curls covering her mound. Leaning in, he nuzzled between her inner thighs, his nose bumping the entrance to her core and with a low growl, he breathed her scent in deep, his claws slicing free then retracting. "You smell like warm honey and something very, very nice. My bear is clawing for a taste."

"Just remember, whatever you do to me, I intend to do in return." Palms flattened to the slick rock wall behind her, she reveled in the spray of cool water washing over her. No steam. No fire.

Finlay continued to rise, just as he had the first time they'd joined, his hands stroking over her hips, her belly, his fingertips brushing the undersides of her breasts. Each of his touches sent a bolt of raw heat racing through her. Finlay would claim her, make her his in every way, and nothing could have brought her more joy than being here with him, right now.

Hands sliding up along the smooth, sheer rock wall, she gave herself completely to him as he peeled her shift higher. His lengthy cock, so hard and full, the head escaping his loosened waistband and poking out, made her body sing for closer contact. She lifted one leg, wrapped it around the back of his legs and tugged him closer. "This mated bond is so wonderful."

"And all-consuming." He rubbed against her, his entire body as slick and wet as hers as he swept her shift over her head and touched his lips to hers. "You're so beautiful, your skin so creamy and soft." He flapped her undergarment onto the ledge, shoved his pants down his thickly muscled legs and laid the leather down as another barrier against them and the stone. Then he swept her up, laid her on top of their clothes and kneeling between her spread legs, captured her breasts in his hands and eased them together. Thumbs swiping her nipples, stiffening them further, he licked around her aureoles, first one and then the other. "So wet and hard. I need more," he rasped.

"Take whatever you desire."

He kissed her again, so deliciously he turned the heat radiating through her blood into a roaring fire, until every inch of her sizzled and every one of her thoughts scattered. She needed this, needed him.

"You're all mine." Greedily, he sucked one nipple deep inside his mouth and played the tip with his tongue.

Delicious heat radiated through her blood and she arched her back, thrust her breasts ever deeper into his exquisite touch and whimpered. "Finlay, I need more."

"I've got you." He rubbed her nub as he continued to lave her breasts and she gasped as white-hot pleasure struck her and rippled outward. She soared as he drove her over the edge, so swiftly and completely, her body so in tune with his touch. Stars shimmered, and ever so slowly, she came back down.

"That was beautiful to watch," he whispered against her ear.

"I want you inside me, now."

"Soon. Your scent has wrapped itself around me and I wish to taste what beckons me below." Grinning, he slid one finger along her wet folds and licked his lips as he eyed her entrance. "Did I do so the first time?"

"Aye, you left no part of me untouched." As he wouldn't this time either. The promise of all that would come shone in his passion-filled gaze.

* * * *

"This is a moment I've craved." Finlay longed for his mate, the only woman he'd ever love. Such a ravenous hunger rolled through him. "I want your scent on my tongue, as well as in and around me. I want to have you so deeply ingrained inside me, that you're as much a part of me as I long to be a part of you."

He slid onto his belly between her knees, raised her legs, hooked them over his shoulders until her bottom lifted off the ledge and she lay fully exposed to him. From the overhead vent, light filtered through even as the storm raged. The lush pinkness of her enticed him. So beautiful, and all his.

With her inner thighs spread, he traced along her folds then plunged one finger inside her. She bucked and moaned, her beaded nipples hardening even further. "I see you like that."

"There is naught you can do that I willnae like."

"Then are you ready for more?" He stroked her harder and faster, rubbing his thumb across her nub until she arched into his touch.

"Aye," she panted, "love me however you please."

He added a second finger then dipped his head and licked her flesh. His bear rumbled in appreciation then he removed his fingers and thrust his tongue inside her, stroked the inside of her channel then retreated and did the same all over again. Lapping her, he built her next orgasm to a peak with his mouth and tongue alone. This was what he wanted, to hear her soft cries for more, to know her passion rose to such heights because of him. A myriad of sensations stormed through him and his cock throbbed, so heavy and full and wanting as he drank at the very heart of his woman.

"Finlay, I cannae take any more. I need your mouth on mine."

"I'm coming, love." He lifted up, licking and nipping her

skin as he did, along the sweet line of her groin, around her belly button and her tasty midsection. Then he gorged himself on her full breasts and her pebbled nipples. Higher still, he moved, along her sweet collarbone and over the soft flesh of her neck. He laved his mark, still as visible as when he'd bitten her earlier in the day, then nibbled on her tiny lobe. All of her became a heady, intoxicating rush he wanted to drown himself in.

"My mouth is here." She cupped the back of his head with one hand and brought his mouth to hers. She kissed him and as she did, she reached one hand down between them, slid her fingers around his cock and pulled him in long strokes. His spine tingled and the pressure in his shaft built swiftly.

Kissing her, savoring the luscious recesses of her mouth, and having her hand on him had his cock begging for release. He had to take her, join their bodies and never let go. He gave into that need and blood pounding, plunged his cock deep inside her.

The fiery heat of her core bathed him in her scent and she moaned into his mouth, clutched his butt and pulled him in even deeper. *"This is where you belong, my warrior, my lover, the other half of my soul."*

"We're one, and from this moment forth, we shall always be so." Ever so slowly, he slid back out then pushed all the way inside her again, every inch of her welcoming heat accepting him. *"I want to make you come, over and over. Keep your mind open to mine and share all you feel."*

"I feel too much, yet also no' nearly enough. This time we come together." With her mind open to his and her legs looped around the backs of his knees, she clung to him. *"Make me fly."*

"I love you, Arabel, with all that I am." He thrust, pounding into her and as he did, he sucked the skin of her neck between his lips and guided her mouth to his neck with one hand behind her head.

She rocked with him as he moved, razzed her teeth over his fiercely beating pulse and as he sensed her spiraling need to mark him through their merged minds, he bit down and so did she.

"*Bite me again*," he demanded, bucking into her, his pace wild, driven by the very heart of his bear. She met each of his thrusts with one of her own and bit him on the other side of his neck. He roared his pleasure and bit her a second time and as her inner muscles tightened and dragged him in, euphoria overwhelmed him and he spilled his essence deep inside her.

"Finlay, I wish for your seed to take root and give me a child." She stroked his back. "I never believed such a thing would ever be possible, but now everything has changed. I have you, for the rest of my life."

"As I have you, and if you wish my child, then I won't rest until I give you a babe all of your own."

Theirs was such a perfect union, his shifter soul connecting and locking tight with hers. She was his, the only one he'd ever desire, and he'd ensure from this moment forth, he never let her go. No more lost memories. Never again.

* * * *

Pleasure swept through Arabel as the cool mist continued to drift over her. Never had she ever expected to join with a man and be able to hold him close for the rest of her life. This was the most magical gift and her man, the most enchanting being she could ever have dreamed of. "'Tis my turn on top. I wish to see how else we might join."

"I don't wish to leave your body." His enjoyment flowed through their merged link.

"I promise to make things even more enjoyable for you." She pushed against his broad shoulders although he budged not an inch. "Please."

"Well, that was the magic word." He rolled smoothly over on their clothing, every inch of his body still fully aligned with hers and his shaft stirring and lengthening again deep within her.

"You feel so strong and full inside me. I love having you deep within."

"I'm sure I love it more." He caressed her bottom and rocked his hips, his cock sliding even deeper inside. "Kiss me, my sweet."

"No' yet. This is my chance to touch you as I please." She pushed herself up into a seated position, and mesmerized by his honed muscles, stroked his sculpted chest. She skated along the enticing path of his glorious abs then lower still, until she reached behind her and cupped his balls. "Oh, that's very nice."

"Your position suits me rather well too." His golden eyes smoldered as he traced one lone finger around her nipple then he lifted up onto his elbows and kissed her, his tongue sweeping over hers in a hot, languorous caress.

Her body clenched so tight she almost came from his kiss alone. "You are going to make the perfect husband."

"Aye, my fire-wielder, until the end of time." He toppled her over onto her back and thrust inside her with one powerful stroke.

The impact of their fast joining had her fighting to hold onto her control. She would get her chance to touch her mate as she pleased at some point, and luckily, she had a lifetime of such promising moments ahead of her. She'd been bound to him across the centuries, and now that he'd found her, she never intended to let him go.

Her mate. Her bear. Her very heart and soul.

Chapter 14

Far into the future, Murdock Matheson stood at his solar window on the second floor of Matheson Castle overlooking the inner courtyard. A new day had dawned, one overflowing with an abundance of hope. Farther along the loch where the fae village had once stood, ruins now graced the land rather than dust. Their fae people had survived, and this morning when he'd shared the news with his clansmen, they'd cheered.

He'd then contacted Finlay's parents at Ivanson Castle, and Michael and Megan had been thrilled to learn their son had now found his mate and the battle to save the fae village had been won. They'd asked him to keep them informed of any visions to come and he'd assured them he would. They also longed for their sons to return, but not until their mission was complete. At least now, their shifter clan no longer stood on the precipice of extinction.

Aye, come the next full moon, those who still remained unmated might feel the urge to seek out their mate, a dream he now held for his men. The 'power of three,' as well as their chosen ones had changed their future and set it on a new and exciting path.

Outside in the training yard, his men attired in pants and shirts battled with renewed vigor. Swords clashed and glinted in the brilliant sunshine. Dust rose from their booted feet as they circled each other and fought, while overhead, a seagull squawked, flew in a wide circle then breezed in to land on the branch of the ancient elm tree scraping against the thick stone walls of the keep.

His vision fluttered, and he closed his eyes.

A barrage of images burst to dazzling life and he grasped ahold of them.

A beaming Finlay in tan pants and a billowy white shirt knocked on Iain and Isla's chamber door, a glowing Arabel in a full-skirted ruby gown at his side.

Iain, in his belted plaid, opened the door and smiled at his brother. "Well, well, it's good to see you looking so happy. You've been gone for days. Come in." He motioned them inside and shut the door after them. "Although I could sense your contentment through our bond so I wasn't worried, not in the least."

"As I sensed the same contentment." Kirk, his smile as wide as Iain's, slapped his black leather-covered thighs as he rose from the corner navy padded chair and grasped Finlay's forearm. "I take it you two have found a way to join together without the need for a storm?"

"We have. We tested the theory after the storm passed and discovered we can replicate the four elements with ease. The wind still blew down the tunnel into the cavern, and I lit a fire in place of lightning. We were covered for water with the mist and pool, and with the earth, we were well underground. We are each other's match in every way." Finlay clutched Kirk's forearm in return and Iain's with his other hand. "On our return, we'll build our own underground home close to Ivanson Castle and ensure we have all we need on hand."

"And we'll aid you since you'll no likely want that done as soon as possible." Iain chuckled as he gripped Finlay and Kirk's forearms, their circle of three complete as they stood together, each facing the other.

"I'm so happy for you both." Isla squealed as she rushed across the room in a flurry of burgundy skirts and hugged Arabel.

Arabel squeezed Isla back. "None with my skill have ever known of this alignment needed of the four elements in order to exhaust our fire, and we are lucky to have discovered that is all that's needed to be together as we wish. 'Tis wonderful to know there is naught any fire-wielder in the future must give up." She glanced at Kirk and smiled. "'Tis now time for you to find your chosen one. The 'power of three' arena complete without their mates and you are the last."

"Last, but not the least, and the next full moon is mere days away. That should aid me in my search since so far it's been to no avail." Determination slashed Kirk's face. "I intend to find my woman and I won't cease until I have."

"Here, here," Finlay cheered. "We're not leaving this time until the 'power of three' rings with the greatest strength it can, that of all three of us joining with our chosen ones."

"Aye, and I pledge my promise of aid wherever and however it is needed." Arabel ducked under Finlay's outstretched hold with his brothers and wrapped her arms around his waist. On her toes in the center of the circle, she kissed his chin. "You can always rely on me."

"I pledge the same promise, and no one is leaving me behind this time, not once more." Isla slipped underneath Iain's arm and joined Arabel in the center of the three brothers, her compelling words shimmering all around them. She locked gazes with her mate and offered him a cheeky smile. "Am I understood, my big bear?"

"I understand you well, my little bear." He bent and kissed the tip of her nose. "Very, very well."

Murdock chuckled. It appeared no one could tame a fire-wielder or a compeller, not when all they desired to do was stand right beside their men and offer their love and aid. Aye, the 'power of three' was a formidable presence, but made even more so by the highly skilled women who belonged to them.

Now, it was time for Kirk to find his mate, an exciting journey he couldn't wait to see unfold, a journey the 'power of three' would embrace and conquer. Of that he had no doubt.

145

Coming in Highlander's Seduction, Book 3 is Kirk's story.

Author's Note

Clan Matheson descends from a twelfth century man called Gilleoin, a man who was believed to have been from the ancient Royal House of Lorne. The name Matheson has been attributed to the Gaelic words Mic Mhathghamhuim which means "Son of the Bear," and the clan chief's arms carry two bears as supporters. In the twelfth century, clan Matheson settled around the area of Loch Alsh, Loch Carron, and Kintail, and gave their allegiance to clan MacDonald whose chiefs were the Lords of the Isles. Clan Matheson became a large and powerful clan with a force of around two-thousand men, although by the middle of the sixteenth century they'd diminished greatly in size and influence due to the blood feuds raging across the isles at that time. This warring left them to possess less than a third of the original Matheson property on Loch Alsh.

Interestingly, the other main branch of clan Matheson lived near Loch Shin, Sutherland, at this time, and it was when I discovered this piece of vital information that the story I wished to tell of this once mighty clan and the whispers in ancient times of their ability to shift into the form of the bear became clear.

For the purposes of this story, I chose for Gilleoin to have two sons, both when they came of age forced to go their separate ways, one remaining at Loch Alsh and the other traveling farther afield to an area near Loch Shin. Those sons would then lead their own clans, yet would one day once again merge to bring the legend surrounding clan Matheson back to life. It's time for the whispers to reignite. Clan Matheson are the "Son of the Bear."

This story is woven with as much accuracy to the period and locations as possible, although any mistakes made are mine alone.

This book forms part of *The Matheson Brothers* series, and each story within it is stand-alone.

Please feel free to search for any of my other works. I simply adore strong heroines, and have a ton of fun matching them with their honorable alpha heroes.

Also available in paperback
Scottish Historical Romance

Traveling through time…for a Highlander.

Highlander Heat Series

Highlander's Castle, Book One

Highlander's Magic, Book Two

Highlander's Charm, Book Three

Highlander's Guardian, Book Four

Highlander's Faerie, Book Five

Highlander's Champion, Book Six

by Joanne Wadsworth

Looking for more sexy Scottish adventure?

Read on to catch a preview of the next book in
The Matheson Brothers series – Kirk's story.

Highlander's Seduction

The Matheson Brothers, Book Three

by Joanne Wadsworth

Highlander's Seduction

The Matheson Brothers, Book Three

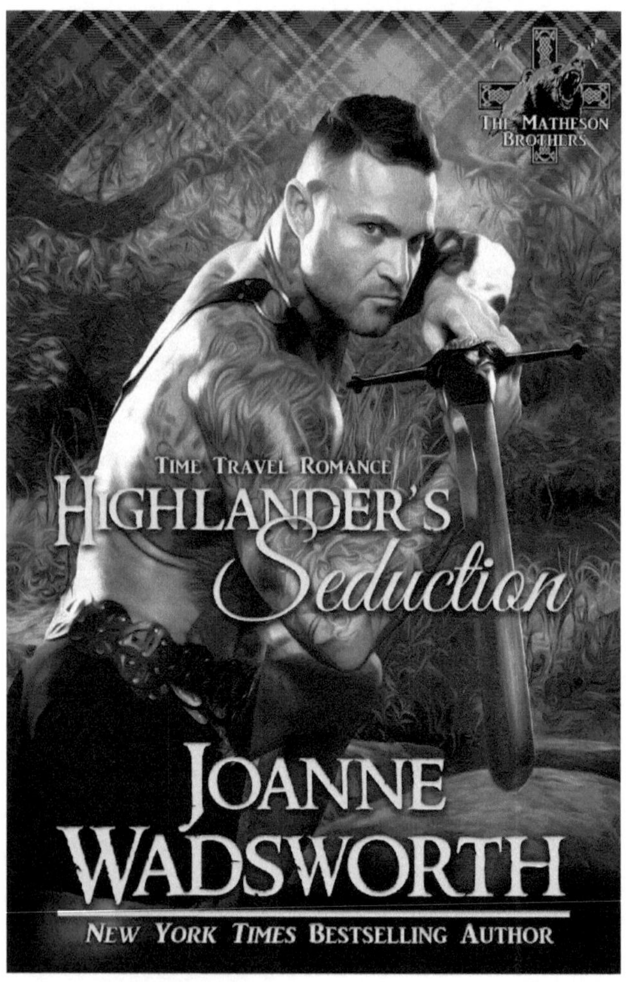

The Seer – Nessa

The ancient House of Clan Matheson, led by Gilleoin, the Chief of Clan Matheson, Scotland, 1210.

Restless and on edge, Nessa strode down the winding stairs from her chamber and entered the great hall. The large vaulted room held a sweeping crown of wooden beamed rafters that rose to an impressive height and within it a hundred or more warriors attired in their clan plaids, clanked tankards of ale together. Lively chatter bubbled forth as her kin feasted on their evening meal. All appeared as it should be, yet still her worry only increased.

She slowed next to the wide arched stone fireplace where sparks flared and firelight shimmered across the hefty clan shield hanging over it. With one finger, she traced along the silver edge where rubies, sapphires and emeralds shone. The jewels surrounded their clan's crest stamped in the center, an image depicting two bears as supporters either side of their chief's arms. Those bears signified what they all fought for—the survival of a loyal race of bear shifters—Gilleoin's line. He was the first, gifted with his ability to shift by The Most High One, and now his twin sons had become the second generation of shifters.

Over twenty years ago when Gilleoin's sons were born, she'd

first spoken the prophecy which would be handed down through the generations, a prophecy that had been unveiled far into the future and with it had brought the recent arrival of travelers from the twenty-first century. Those travelers, three identical warrior brothers of immense strength were known as the 'power of three.' Iain, Finlay, and Kirk could shift shape into the form of the bear, draw claws and roar as Gilleoin and his sons could. Along with them had come Iain's mate, Isla, a woman of dual shifter-fae blood, the daughter of Murdock, her clan's chief and seer.

Even over the wide chasm of centuries separating them, Nessa had come to know Murdock through joint visions and considered him a dear friend. Their beliefs and goals for their people matched, although unfortunately in the future where Murdock lived, Gilleoin's shifter clan now neared extinction and required a new infusion of fae blood within their shifter line if they wished to survive. That infusion was one both she and Murdock intended to see come to fruition, and now with the 'power of three' here in the past, they'd made a start.

At the dais Kirk sat, the youngest of the three warrior brothers, his gaze firm on the tall stained glass window and the setting sun beyond that hovered on the horizon. In the weeks since the three brothers had arrived, Finlay had found Arabel, his chosen one, and joined with her. Now 'twas Kirk's time. He awaited the coming of tonight's full moon to guide him. This was the one night of the month when his shifter senses would lead him directly to her, when his mate would no longer remain beyond his touch or sight.

Kirk clenched his fists as his restlessness mounted. For five long years he'd been searching for his mate but had never found her, not when she resided beyond his future time and instead right here in the past.

As the sun dipped lower, the skies darkened and a quietness suddenly settled over all within the hall.

The full moon rose and Kirk stood, his eyes closed and his

breathing slow as if he settled himself.

Nessa closed her eyes too as the magnitude of the moment rolled through her. As a seer, she'd been gifted with a skill she upheld to the best of her ability, to ensure her clan never faltered, and so too she'd look after Kirk and ensure he found his mate just as his brothers had. She wouldn't fail the 'power of three,' just as they hadn't failed her or their kin here during the recent battle to save the fae village farther along the loch. Because of the 'power of three,' hope now bloomed for their clan as never before.

Images fluttered at the periphery of her mind and a vision flickered into life. A young woman stood at the edge of the fae village's pebbly shore, her white fur cloak wrapped firmly around her. 'Twas Cherub, the faerie king's daughter. She'd never mistake her. Cherub was a close friend and a fae time-walker who was able to cloak her true form and become as one with the very *air* itself by taking on a mist form. Cherub could also sense when two were mated and 'twas her duty to bring those two together. That duty had been one she'd upheld for over a thousand years and across a wide divide of centuries. She was an immortal with flawless skin that sparkled like that of the stars she moved amongst.

Carefully, Nessa focused on Cherub as the lass raised her arms and allowed the wind to bring to her the secrets she needed to unravel. The wind rushed all around Cherub and the fae princess frowned and shook her head as if suddenly confused.

From time to time, Nessa could connect to Cherub when under the weight of a vision and in so doing they could speak to each other. Cherub was one of the few who she talk with in such a way, Murdock the other. She opened up her mind and spoke to Cherub. *"What is wrong, my dear? A vision has shown me you, although I know no' why."*

"Nessa, something is amiss. 'Tis to do with Kirk. I sense who he is mated to, and even though I've always known his mate was fae, this is the first time I've ever sensed exactly who she is."

"And who is his mated one?"

At the dais, a commotion sounded and Nessa opened her eyes.

"I sense her." Kirk pumped a fist into the air, his golden gaze flashing with fierce determination. "She's at the village." Firm words and all within the great hall cheered.

Nessa's vision swirled again and she returned to Cherub. *"Kirk senses his mate."*

"I dinnae know what to do." Cherub paced the beach, her long golden locks swaying about her waist. *"Nessa, I must ask a favor of you. Is it possible for you to keep Kirk from leaving the keep this eve? I need more time."*

"No one can halt a shifter from seeking out his mate, no' even I. Who is his chosen one?"

"Me." A shuddering breath left her lips. *"What am I to do? I cannae take a mate, no' when my duty to my people must come first. They need me, and I cannae forsake them now, no' in these most urgent of times."*

"If you and Kirk are soul bound, then you are each other's match in every way. No matter what your duty is, he is still your destiny."

"Kirk is only one amongst the many who I need to care for." A quiet look of longing crossed Cherub's face. *"I cannae choose him over all others. Look at what happened to Amelia. She is a time-walker and when she took a mate, she gave up her duty. That is something I cannae do."*

"Then what is your intention?"

"I will need to forego the bond, which will be downright difficult. Wish me luck, Nessa. I shall need it." Cherub straightened her shoulders and blew her a kiss. *"We will speak again soon."*

"We shall, although it isnae luck you need, my dear, but to no' forget the depth of the mated bond. There can be only one...for both of you." Nessa blew her a kiss in return and opened her eyes.

Surely the Fae Angel of Love wouldn't be able to turn her mate away. Cherub was the very woman who hunted those who were soul bound and brought them together.

Kirk marched past her and flew out the door. Naught would stop him until he'd found his chosen one. He was a hunter of the most driven sort, which meant now Cherub had become the hunted. Aye, she'd need to keep a close eye on Cherub and Kirk over the coming days. Never would she allow Gilleoin's future line to fall into extinction. The 'power of three' needed to ring with their greatest strength, and for that to occur, all three brothers had to find their mates and complete the bond. Kirk was the last, although not the least.

The Seer – Murdock Matheson

Matheson Castle, led by Murdock Matheson, the Chief of Clan Matheson, a man with dual shifter-fae blood, Scotland, current day.

Murdock Matheson paced the water's edge of Loch Alsh, his current frustration riding him hard. It had been days since his last vision and he detested not seeing his daughter, Isla, and the three warrior brothers known as the 'power of three,' who'd traveled with her over eight-hundred years into the past.

Mere days ago, the 'power of three' along with their mates had successfully saved the fae village from the MacKenzie chief's attack and now their shifter clan held more hope for their future than ever before.

If only he could force a vision. At least Nessa, the seer of ancient times, would be watching over his kin. Of that he had no doubt.

"Chief!" Daniel, his right hand man, jogged along the grassy verge of the loch's shoreline, the castle's fortified stone walls rising high behind him. The thick slabs of gray stone were bathed a glorious golden hue as the sun dipped below the horizon and the moon rose majestically overhead.

"Is all well?"

"More than well." Hands on his hips, Daniel halted and grinned. "Several of our unmated men have reported their senses are stirring as never before. They're certain their chosen ones now await them, although they need to leave tonight and begin their search."

"Inform them that they may and that I wish them well. Certainly if their searches lead them this night to a place where no one awaits them, then it could well mean their mates reside in the past as Finlay and Kirk's mates do. We will need Cherub if that is so." Murdock rarely spoke of Cherub, keeping her secrets as needed. He clapped Daniel on the back. "Ensure all those who need to leave on their search have all they require at hand. This is our time, for our clan to embrace a new future."

"Will do, Chief, and it's a new future we long for." Daniel grasped Murdock's forearm in a firm warrior hold then jogged back toward the keep in his clan plaid.

Aye, a new time had now dawned for their shifter line, one of renewed hope and endless possibilities.

Quietly, he closed his eyes and focused on Nessa.

He couldn't force a vision, but with this level of worry and need consuming him, surely one was close to rising. He'd remain alert if one—

A flurry of images swirled to blazing life and he grasped ahold of them. Nessa stood within the great hall of the ancient House of Clan Matheson in an elegant olive gown, her head bowed under the weight of a vision as her clansmen partook of their evening meal around her. He tapped into her mind and followed the path of her vision.

At the fae village along the loch, a young woman wearing a white fur cloak stood on the pebbly beach. Cherub. He touched his heart. Cherub had visited him from time to time over the years, the very first during his darkest days, not long after he'd lost his wife to cancer only a week following Isla's birth. Lost in his grief, he'd barely been able to care for himself let alone his newborn daughter. Yet he'd promised his wife on her passing that he'd raise their child with all the love and devotion she would have done, a promise he'd kept and would continue to do so.

Cherub had been the one to console him, to assure him his wife awaited him in the land of the fae beyond the veil, in a place that for now would remain beyond his reach, but not forever. One day he would join her, when his time on Earth was done.

"*Murdock?*" Nessa's voice reverberated softly through his mind.

"*I'm here, my friend. How is Isla?*"

"*Your daughter is very well. Iain keeps a close watch over her, as do I. She misses you.*"

"*As I miss her. Tell her I love her. I saw Cherub. She looks troubled.*"

"*She's discovered this eve that she is mated to Kirk, a bond she feels she cannae allow to take due to her duty.*"

Cherub was devoted to those of fae blood who walked this Earth. She ensured each and every one of her people found their soul bound mate, even though they might be separated by a divide of time. She could command the very *air* itself and open portals in time. He drew his focus back to the young woman who held a special place in his heart and always would. Just as he could communicate with Nessa during a vision, so too he could do so with Cherub when his sight led him to her. "*Cherub, how are you?*"

"*I am well, Murdock.*" A smile lifted Cherub's lips. "*How are you?*"

"*I have good news. Several of my men have just reported sensing their mates, for the first time.*"

"*Many of them shall be led to a place this eve where their mate should be, but they willnae find who they search for. No' when their mates reside here in this time. The same will have occurred for the other shifter clan farther across the Highlands. I need you to speak to their chief, Michael. Let him know the Fae Angel of Love's duty stands firm and always shall."*

"I'll inform him. Michael's been eager to hear more news about Iain, Finlay and Kirk. He misses his sons and will be pleased to hear of your bond taking form with Kirk."

"I'm afraid I cannae accept the bond with my mate, no' if I wish to aid all those who will soon need me. Kirk is but one of many."

"No one has ever been able to defy the mated bond."

"Then I shall attempt to be the first."

"There is no need for you to deny what should be."

"There is every need if I'm to continue to care for my people." Warmth radiated from her through their link and enveloped him. *"We shall speak again soon. Your clan shall need me in the coming days and I willnae forsake you, or them. Of that I give you my word."*

"Then take care, my friend, for I too shall be watching over you."

"Until the next time." Cherub's image fluttered away, as did his vision and his connection to Nessa.

The fae time-walker was devoted to each and every one of her people, her work usually done in secret. He only hoped she was as devoted to caring for herself as well. There was strength in allowing the mated bond and joining with the one who was always meant to be theirs. Aye, a mated pair should never be separated, not even when duty stood in their way.

Chapter 1

At the fae village, farther along the loch from the ancient House of Clan Matheson, Scotland, 1210.

Under a darkening sky, Cherub paced the pebbly beach before the fae village, the wind whistling around her. It flapped her white fur cloak back from her shoulders and whipped her blond hair in a frenzy. High above, the full moon rose and bathed the Earth in its heavenly glow. This one night of the month always offered such promise to those who were mated, yet this eve, it brought only longing to her very soul, a longing that would soon be crushed. She couldn't forsake her fae-blooded kind, not when so many would now need her aid in seeking out their mated one.

"Papa!" A lad dashed through the gate in the high stone wall surrounding the village and raced toward the foaming water's edge. 'Twas Joseph, Amelia's son. Wearing loose-legged tan breeches two inches too short on his legs and a long green tunic, Joseph swung a wooden pail in his hand as he hurried along the grassy trail.

Ten years ago, Amelia, the second of only three time-walkers born to their people, had traveled from the future to the past and become soul bound to Olaf here in this time. When their bond had taken form, her friend had chosen to forego her skill and devote herself to her mate. That had left Cherub as the only one to care for their Earthbound fae, the third time-walker caring for those beyond the veil. Still, 'twas a duty Cherub adored and one she'd never forsake.

"Wait there, Joseph." Beyond the choppy breakers, Olaf waved from his skiff then hauled his nets in. He rowed into shore, bounded out and roped his boat to a boulder. Joseph handed him the pail and Olaf filled it with his catch before the two of them walked back along the beach toward her. With a smile, Olaf stopped and gazed at her. "How are you this eve, Cherub?"

"I'm very well. How is Amelia?"

"A little anxious following the recent battle on these shores. 'Tis good to see you're back."

"I can never stay away from my kin here for long." Thankfully she'd only been gone a short time. Bending, she rustled Joseph's windblown brown locks. "Tell your mama I shall visit her soon, now that I've returned to this time."

"I will." Joseph ogled her sparkly skin. "Mama said she saw your papa beyond the veil, and more than once when she traveled there. She said the king's skin glitters too."

"Aye, his does. Each eldest child born within the royal line holds such sparkly skin as mine." She was one of seven, the eldest of all her siblings. She kissed Joseph's cheek. His mother was like a sister to her, and Joseph was the first and only child born to a time-walker. Like his mother, he too would be an immortal, his soul having been blood bound to Amelia's through his birth.

Olaf wrapped an arm around Joseph's shoulder. "I've caught plenty of fish this eve, Cherub. Are you able to join us for the evening meal?"

"I wish I could, but there is a man I must wait here to meet. My thanks though for your kind invitation."

"Then you must come as soon as you can. Amelia misses you."

"As I miss her. Tell her I shall visit on the morrow."

"I will. Take care." Olaf squeezed her arm then led Joseph up the trail and through the gate into the village. Amelia and her kin were so happy here, and she too couldn't have been happier for them. Joseph was a treasure, a child who brought such delight to one and all who met him.

With a soft sigh, she turned her gaze back toward Matheson House. This coming encounter was one that tore at her. She was to meet her soul bound mate and then turn him away. Life wasn't fair, but then that she'd learnt well over the centuries.

Down the trail toward the sea-gate landing, a warrior with midnight black locks brushing his shoulders ran. He bounded aboard a skiff, released the mooring rope then coiled and stored it under the center seat. With the oars in hand, he rowed.

Once he cleared the bay, he tucked his oars away and raised the sail. The wind filled it with a hearty slap and with his feet braced wide along one side and the ropes in hand, he steered the skiff as it shot off like an arrow toward her.

Her fae senses reached out toward his and butterflies abounded in her belly. Kirk's drive to reach the village was honed completely in on her, the one woman who was meant to be his, and the one woman she intended to deny him of. Finding his chosen one had consumed him these past five years, just as it had his two identical brothers who'd now found their mates. Although never once had she known that 'twas her Kirk searched for. If only she had, then she could have let him down far sooner and thus allowed him to move on and enjoy his life.

The wind plastered Kirk's billowy white tunic against his muscled chest and sent the sword holstered at his side swaying. He would be here within a minute or two and there was naught more she could do now but anxiously await his arrival.

Over her shoulder, the need of those within the houses of stone and clay cloistered so tightly together called out to her and touched her very heart. Throughout the days and years to come, so many would need her aid and that knowledge firmed her stance. Their people couldn't lose another time-walker, a fact she hoped her mate could accept.

With her decision made, she dissolved into a mist and became as one with the very air itself, the element she commanded. 'Twas best Kirk not have her image in his mind. If he did, then that would make their parting all the more harder.

Kirk steered his skiff toward land, lowered the sail as he neared the shore and jumped into the knee-deep water. He hauled his boat onto the beach and in snug black leather pants, marched toward her. He strode past her then stopped and swung about. With a determined slash to his lips and his nose to the air, he breathed deep and prowled back. In a wide circle, he moved, each of his steps drawing him closer and closer to her unseen position.

"Why can't I see you, my elusive imp? I'm finally here in the right time and place and I should be able to." He halted directly in front of her, lifted one hand and swept it in a wide arc.

His hand passed right through her, and her very soul shimmered with need.

"Where are you?" he whispered into the wind, raw pain in his voice.

Her heart ached with what could never be. A soul bound match was what she sought for others, believed in to the greatest degree. "I'm so sorry, Kirk. You have my sincerest apologies for withholding myself from you." She allowed her voice to flow to him. Leaving him wondering about her wasn't something she'd ever be able to do, not to the man her very soul had now been bound to. "You and I, and this mated bond that has formed between us, it cannae be."

"You know my name?" He searched where she stood.

"I do, and that is because 'tis now emblazoned on my heart."

"Why can't I see you?"

"I'm a time-walker, one of only three who can command the very air itself. 'Tis my element and if I wish, so too I can become as one with it."

"Why would you withhold yourself from me?"

"I…" She wavered in her stance and took form, although she remained fully cloaked and unseen. "You can touch me now if you wish."

He swept one hand out, his fingers sliding through her locks then slowly, he brought his hand to his chest, his fist clenched around a long strand of her pale blond hair. "Thank you."

"My name is Cherub. I am also the one who hears the whispers between souls who arena yet aligned so that I might bring them together across time, no matter where they might be."

"You're the Fae Angel of Love?" Surprise widened his eyes. "I've heard of you, or I should say the legend. Tales spoken of the Fae Angel of Love give our clan hope."

"I'm more than just a tale. I was born to serve my people and have done so for over a thousand years." She looked into his eyes and almost drowned in his stunning golden gaze. A shifter's eyes, although there was more. They were rimmed with a glimmer of starburst yellow, adding a spark of heat that sent another bout of butterflies flittering about in her belly. "So many seek my aid, and my duty is to those of fae blood who walk this Earth."

"I'm one of Ivan's direct descendants, Gilleoin's second-born son, and unlike Gilleoin's firstborn line, our clan is shifter alone. I have no fae blood."

"Aye, 'tis true your clan does no' hold any fae skills as the firstborn son's line does, yet Sorcha's blood still flows through your line all the same." Sorcha, Gilleoin's wife and Nessa's daughter was a strongly skilled fae who held the ability of aura reading. "That trace of fae blood, although diluted over the centuries, is still enough to call to me." She cupped his cheek, her lips lifting. "I have spoken to Isla's father, Murdock, this night and he has informed me that many of the unmated men in his clan now sense their chosen ones. The same will have occurred for your clan farther across the Highlands from him. I also asked him to speak to your father and to let Michael know I will watch over one and all, just as I've always done."

"As I intend to now watch over you." He slid his hand gently over hers and closed his eyes. "I want my mate, the one woman who was always meant to mine. I want you, Cherub. Please, show yourself fully to me. Uncloak."

His demand to see her tugged at her heart and caused her to sway toward him, to falter for a mere moment in her stance. She should walk away from him now, and before any ties between their souls began to weave together.

"I'm sorry. That I cannae do."

"Legend says the Fae Angel of Love is the faerie king's firstborn child."

"Aye, I am." She stroked her fingers back and forth over his skin. Touching him, even for this stolen moment in time, soothed her very soul. "You must understand, there is too much at stake for me to allow our joining. So many others need me."

"As I now need you too. Surely you can take one night off from your duties. Aren't you curious at all about who I am and why a bond has taken between us? Give me some time." He smoothed his hand over her wrist and up her arm then slid his fingers under her hair and around her nape. "I'm so incredibly curious about you. I've wondered for five long years just who you were, as well as craved the thought of getting to know you. You can't leave me now."

She should move away, yet his hold, so deliciously tender, and the sheer look of desire in his gaze even though he couldn't see her kept her rooted to the spot. "I've never once sensed I was bound to another. Five years may have passed for you, but for me, only a few minutes have."

"I see." He found her other arm then swept down to her hand and threaded their fingers together. "I understand your dilemma. I certainly don't wish to see my fellow kin lose the chance of being brought to their mated one. Holding hope is all that the men in our shifter line hold onto, and now I've found you, I too have no intention of losing that hope. There must be a way around all of this, so that both of us can receive what we need to from our bond."

"My duty is all-consuming, barely allowing me any time for myself, let alone a mate."

"Then allow me to aid you. I needn't be a burden but a partner to share the load." Slowly, he lowered to one knee, brought her hand to his lips and pressed a soft kiss against her palm. "Cherub, from this day forth, I give you my oath. All I desire is to keep you safe, to honor your needs above my own. Allow me to stand at your side, to aid you in your duty. I'll do all I can to ensure you never falter in caring for your people."

A slow heat invaded her limbs and spread in a rippling wave through her body. His words touched her heart. "You shouldnae have made such a vow to me."

"My word is absolute and I won't take it back. Meeting you is all I've ever dreamed of, and the thought of you leaving me because your duty is so all-consuming tears my very soul in two. Give me a chance. Allow me to prove I speak the truth and will never fail you." He rose to his feet, scooped her into his arms and walked with her toward the forest rising high behind the village. The tops of the pine trees swayed in the breeze and an owl hooted from deep within.

"Where are you taking me?" She looped her arms around his neck and held on as he strode along the trail into the darkening forest.

"There is a special place not far from here, one I discovered not long after my arrival. I'd like to take you there. Give me this one night. Don't leave me or forego our bond until you've given me the chance to prove my vow was spoken in truth. I would forever honor it, and you."

Goodness. If she granted his request and spent one night with him, would she then be able to walk away from him once the sun had risen in the morning? Soul bound mates would do anything for each other. That she'd witnessed time and time again over the centuries, although Amelia had still stood down from her duty after accepting the bond with Olaf. That she couldn't allow to have happen to her.

"You've gone very quiet all of a sudden. Does that mean you agree to one night?"

He asked for so little and right now no other needed her. "I'll give you one night, although no more."

"Thank you." He buried his nose in her hair and grinning, drew in a deep breath. "Mmm, you smell delicious, like fresh air and an ocean breeze. Where do you live, Cherub?"

"My place is here on Earth, amongst those of fae blood, wherever that might be and whatever century that draws me to." In truth, she owned several parcels of land, had built a home on one such plot and favored it as a home base. She also kept a chamber right here at Matheson House, one Nessa insisted she use as often as she needed to, which would be greatly needed during the coming days and weeks ahead now so many shifters in the future would be seeking their mates here in this time. "You can put me down if you wish. I've agreed to one night and I'll gladly walk with you."

"Thanks for the offer but I'd rather hold onto you." He strode along a leaf-strewn path, the canopy high and thick above and blocking all sign of the moon. "You feel so good in my arms."

"Do you carry women about often?" He was rather adept at it.

"No." He chuckled. "You are and will be the only woman I'll ever hold close to my heart. That I promise you. So too my bear is also feeling restless this eve and demands this touch. Releasing you right now would be impossible."

"'Tis a shame I willnae get to meet your bear. Is his pelt the same color as your hair?" His black locks were as dark as a midnight sky.

"I'll show you my bear, if you uncloak and show me your true form. Shall we make a deal?"

"Nay, no deal." It appeared her mate liked to negotiate.

"Do you hear that?" Kirk cocked one ear.

Up ahead, the sea crashed against the high cliffs and the sound traveled to her. Kirk was taking her toward the isolated bay farther along the inner channel of the loch, one of the few places she too adored. "I do." She touched his jaw and turned his gaze from the trail to hers. His golden eyes glinted in the dark. "We are headed to one of my favorite places."

"I wish I could see you." He searched her gaze. "What color are your eyes, my mate?"

"They're blue, a very plain and dull blue."

"There is no shade of blue that is plain or dull." A low branch loomed and he ducked his head, his lips brushing her cheek as he kept her from scraping against it as well. "I can feel you're clothed in a fur cape. What else do you wear?"

She grasped the edges of her fluttering cloak and tucked the fur tighter about her. "Just clothes."

"You're so elusive. Come on. You must give me a hint. He nuzzled her neck, his nose buried deep in her hair. "I'll forever wonder otherwise."

"They're clothes which keep me warm no matter where I might travel." She touched a finger to his lower lip and swept to one raised corner then back again to the center. He had such soft lips, and when his tongue darted out and he licked her finger, she gasped.

"Mmm, I see you're elusive and tasty." He strode uphill, stepped over a fallen log barring their way and along the winding trail toward the cliff top that overlooked the bay.

She tucked her head into his shoulder and rubbed her cheek against the thin white cotton of his tunic. The deep V collar was loosely laced and she slipped her hand inside his shirt and stroked his golden skin. The need to touch one's mate was natural and she didn't fight that desire. So too she'd agreed to one night, so she may as well allow herself this moment of release. "You feel warm, almost too warm."

"That's because my shifter blood runs hotter than most, and right now it's been a couple of days since I last shifted. Heat builds to a higher degree when I'm overdue for the Change." He emerged at the top of the cliff overlooking the curve of the bay below. Moonlight glimmered across the white-capped waves rolling onto the white sand beach, turning them a stunning silvery hue.

This bay held a touch of magic, was only accessible by a tunnel in the cliff at the base. Few knew of the hidden entrance, which ensured this protected place remained so very private and pristine.

"You said before you're one of only three who holds command over the element of air. Where are the other two time-walkers located?"

"Jeremiah's duty is to the full-blooded fae beyond the veil. He rarely has time to aid me on Earth. The last is Amelia, one of my dearest friends. We are close, like sisters in truth."

"Where does Amelia's duty lie, here or beyond the veil?" With care, he traversed the edge of the cliff where it led downward toward the secret entrance. On one side, the odd stone rattled loose under his feet and clacked down the side of the sheer rock wall, while on the other, the rough branches of the swaying pine trees brushed his arms.

"Amelia used to aid me here on Earth, but she stood down from her duty ten years ago when she became soul bound with Olaf. They live at the village and have a son named Joseph. He's the first child to be born to a time-walker and such a delight. He also holds the skill of foreknowledge, an ability similar to a seer's although still a little different."

"I've not met Amelia or Olaf. Is she too an immortal as you are?" He reached the base of the cliff, lowered her to her feet and with their fingers twined together, brushed aside a clump of trailing ivy covering the slim opening in the rock wall. Keeping ahold of her, he edged through the thin gap and weaved along the dark tunnel.

"She is. Amelia's mate is also an immortal, as is their child."

"How is Olaf an immortal?"

"A time-walker, once they take a mate, can hold their chosen one's soul to theirs. Amelia spoke a spell which bound a piece of Olaf's soul to hers, so like her, he too will never sicken or age. They will walk the same path for the rest of their lives, together as one."

"That's a beautiful thing."

"It is." They reached the end of the tunnel and emerged before the beach. She jumped free onto the soft sand and twirled around, her feet digging in deep. This secluded bay with its thin strip of white sand always took her breath away.

"Cherub?" Kirk swept his hands through the air as he searched for her. "Where are you?"

"I'm right here." She twirled around again. "I love this place."

"As soon as I stumbled upon it, I felt as if I'd come home. There's a secluded bay very similar to this one at Loch Shin, a place I'm often drawn to, and a place that's only a few hours' drive from my home at Ivanson Castle." He glanced at the sand she'd kicked up then followed her movement and caught her in his arms. His hands slid underneath the flapping sides of her cloak and around her back. Caressing her, he swept down her sides and over her waist. A grin lifted his lips. "You're wearing a silk gown. What color?"

"The gown is white, as is my cape. 'Tis one of my favorite colors. Have you truly been drawn to Loch Shin?" She raised her hands to the glittering jewel of the darkened sky above and leaned back, allowing him to take her full weight as she did.

"During these past five years my search for you has only ever led me in and around that area, more times than not to a place called Angel Bay along the loch's shores. Is that place special to you at all?"

"Oh my." The home she'd built and considered a base rested high on the cliffs overlooking Angel Bay.

"Is that an aye?" He sank to the sand and took her with him as he laid down.

"I—I—" Speaking a mistruth to him tore at her. Instead, she tucked one errant lock of his hair behind his ear and said, "I enjoy visiting Angel Bay, just as I enjoy visiting this place. Both bring me comfort, as well as allow me to walk the shoreline in complete seclusion."

"Hmm, why do I feel as if you're not quite telling me the whole truth?" He removed his sword belt, set it beside him then with his warm hands on her hips, brought her back against him. Gently, he smoothed one hand along her outer thigh then tucked her top leg snugly between his leather-clad legs, their bodies in complete alignment from head to toe. She wasn't surprised by his move, or his need to hold her close. Those who were soul bound required touch on a deeper level to most. He skimmed up her arm and swept one finger along her gown's low-cut neckline. "Can you explain a little more?"

"Nay, I dinnae wish to encourage your pursuit and explaining more will do so."

"Ha." He chuckled. "You're my mate, the one woman I will always pursue, and there is nothing you can say or do to cease that encouragement." He caught her cheeks in his hands and traced his thumbs under her eyes and over her nose. He smoothed along her jaw, over her chin then slowly delved across her lips. His breath stuttered and he leaned in, pressed his forehead against hers. "You have the smoothest, softest skin."

"I have no' aged past my twentieth year even though I've lived over a thousand years." A gentle sea breeze whispered around them, lifted his shirt hem and gave a glimpse of his tanned abs. His black pants hung low on his hips and the leather clung to his powerful thighs. She lifted her gaze back to his and almost drowned in the deep desire reflecting back at her. She palmed his chest, his heart thundering under her hand. A simple walk was leading to so much more—more she couldn't currently turn away from.

"Cherub, I wish for a kiss. Would that be permissible?"

"I dinnae think—"

"Thinking is currently not permitted." He lowered his mouth to her, his lips so aching soft as he joined them together, then he deepened their kiss and licked her tongue, his breath mingling seductively with hers.

Aye, thinking shouldn't be permitted. Why not live in the moment, even if only for one night? Granting herself at least that much, settled her deep inside. Gently, she sucked his lower lip into her mouth then indulged in her need for more. She kissed him, deeply, then grasped his shoulders and pulled him fully on top of her, his heavenly weight exactly what she needed. She melted into the sand, reveling in his warm spicy scent as it surrounded and embedded itself into her. "I like your kisses, Kirk."

"I'm sure I could convince you to like a whole lot more of me if you were only open to the possibility."

"I also like your intriguing mind." She kissed him again and he kissed her back. In all the centuries that had passed her by, never had she taken one stolen moment like this and kept it all to herself. Being with him right now was all she desired.

"This could get rather addictive, rather fast." He lifted his head and grinned at her, and she grinned right back, not that he could see her smile. "Don't you think so, my elusive imp?"

"Very addictive and also very wrong." She sank her hands into his hair and raked her nails lightly across his scalp. "Kirk, I dinnae wish for you to live a lonely life, so should you wish to join with another—I mean—you shouldnae miss out on all life has to offer just because your soul was bound to the wrong woman."

"You are the perfect woman for me, and I've already given

you my vow. I will not forsake it." He rubbed his nose against hers. "You also need to give me something to hold onto, to keep my hope alive, that you might one day change your mind. Give me your promise in return, Cherub, that you'll at least consider allowing our bond to take."

"I cannae." She shook her head, and he pressed his palms to her cheeks and followed her movement.

"I see. You're going to be a stubborn mate."

"I am not a stubborn mate but a wise one." She palmed the back of his head and brought his mouth back to within a breath of hers. "I also wish for another kiss."

"So do I. Of at least that we're in complete agreement on." He swooped in and kissed her, taking her breath away with his passion. He was a seduction she desired more of and she couldn't help but give into her current need. Living a thousand years alone hadn't been easy. 'Twas time to give into her destiny, even if only for this one night.

* * * *

Kirk kissed Cherub with all the longing he'd held deep inside him these past five years. He caressed her sides, roamed down and gripped her hips. He rolled them both until she came up on top of him, her cape sweeping his sides and her hood falling softly over her head. Within the cocoon of fur, he caught a glimmer of her features, one delicate earlobe, the partial sight dazzling and making him blink. Did her skin sparkle? Or was that just his imagination? Hell, he longed to see more of her, to have her fully uncloak herself, but so too he also understood her desire not to. She worried that in allowing their mated bond to take form, her calling to bring those who were soul bound together would no longer take precedence. Only she didn't know him. He'd do all he could to aid her. Never would he hold her back from her duty.

"Mmm, Kirk." She murmured his name against his lips then kissed him again, so deeply and completely he fell into her silken web. Nowhere else did he desire to be other than right here with her. She scattered each and every one of his thoughts, so swiftly and decisively. All that roared through his mind was the need to mate, to mark his chosen one and to never let her go.

"I need more, Cherub."

"I cannae allow a joining."

"I understand, but surely you can allow me to see to your needs and mine, or at least to take the edge of this hunger riding us." The front tie of her cape tickled his neck and he groped for the elusive ribbon, tugged it loose and pushed her cloak from her. As soon as the fur left her body, it became exposed to his sight in the moonlight. Eyes closed, he used every one of his bear's senses to its fullest extent to memorize what he could of her. Her scent, fresher than the air itself, embedded itself deeply within him. He wanted to smother her in his own scent, to ensure all who came near her knew she belonged to him. Nuzzling her neck, he licked over her thumping pulse. The deep desire to bite her as his shifter kind did raced through his blood until it became an unstoppable beat.

One night. She'd promised him this one night, and he intended to make it the most memorable one she'd ever known. Following that, he'd continue to convince her of his pure intentions.

A low rumble vibrated in his chest as he pressed himself against her and sucked on her offered skin. She was all woman, and all his. "I need to bite you, and for you to bite me in return. Mark me as yours, Cherub."

"It will mean naught."

"Not to me it won't." He palmed the back of her head and held her mouth to his neck. As he did, he licked her erratic pulse point in the same spot.

"I shouldnae be doing this, only I cannae think straight right now." She clutched his shoulders, her nails digging into his flesh then she shoved his collar to the side and exposed his skin.

"Don't think about anything, only about doing." He razzed

her skin with his teeth then bit her.

"Oooh, that I like." She arched into him, then dipped her head and sank her teeth into his skin in return.

Arousal hit him hard and fast.

"More, I need more." She rocked against him and likely the same surge of desire raced through her as it did through him. Their bite wasn't just a mark of claim but also a bite that brought on fierce sexual desire.

"If I do anything you don't like, then tell me." Slowly, he eased his hand inside the fabric of her bodice, the silk sliding sensuously across the back of his hand. He palmed her full breast and thumbed her peaking nipple. He needed to taste her. Gently, he eased the fabric over her shoulder and exposed her breast. He certainly damn well wished he could see her. Swiftly, he drew the bud deep inside his mouth and played the tip with his tongue. She tasted exquisite, and as he imbibed on her, she clung to him and pushed the sweet morsel even deeper into his mouth. He couldn't halt his desire, didn't even have the chance of doing so. He freed her other breast from its silken bond and gave it as much attention as he'd laved on the first.

"Dinnae stop. Bite me again, Kirk."

"I'd love to." He nipped the upper swell of her breast as he swept upward then sucked on the sensitive skin where her shoulder and neck met. "Ready?"

"Aye, I'm beyond ready."

He bit down and she cried out, her gasp so sweet, as if she was on the brink of an orgasm. Damn it. If she was close, he intended to take her right over the edge and to the heights he desired for her to soar. Everything within him demanded he see to her every need. She'd given up her life for the care of her people, and he would do the same in a heartbeat for her as well. He rolled her onto her side, patted down her body and scrunched her gown's hem up.

Even though he'd never touched a woman before, he

certainly wasn't unaware of what she'd need in order to reach the heights of ecstasy. Few would be who lived in his time. He slid his palm along her inner thigh and nudged her legs farther apart. She widened them and her heat and honey scent called to him. At the entrance to her core, he halted, his fingertips touching the soft curls guarding her most private place. "I need to touch you," he rasped. "Deep inside. May I?"

"Kissing you is clearly dangerous." Softly whispered words as the ties of his pants loosened at her invisible touch. "I've lived a long time, past, future and present included and there is little I'm unaware of that can happen between a man and a woman. I mean, I've never slept with a man, but if you touch me right now then I intend to touch you in return. I want to give you what you desire, or at least what I can for this one night."

"I desire you and whatever you need."

"And I desire the same for you, Kirk. Touch me." She wrapped her hand around his cock and he nearly exploded at her touch right then and there.

"I'm all yours. Touch me too, as you please." He eased his fingers between her folds and rubbed her slick nub. "And I mean for all time, Cherub, not just this one night. You're my mate, the only woman I'll ever touch, the only woman I'll ever desire."

Her need called to him, her sweet scent swirling seductively around him. All he wanted to do was wriggle down, flip her skirts higher and imbibe at the very heart of her. His bear fairly raged at him to do so. Instead he plunged one finger inside her hot channel and bumped his nose against hers as he tried to find her lips.

"I'm right here." She angled her head and captured his mouth and kissed him, just as ravenously as he kissed her. She was the only one who could provide him with the ultimate sustenance he needed.

Aye she was his one and all, the only woman his soul would ever seek. He stroked deep inside her then pulled out to caress her clit, his desire to give her everything she needed roaring through him.

"Oh, that feels sooo good. Dinnae stop." She worked his cock in long pulls then swiped her thumb over the head. His cock wept for more and he pushed deeper into her delicious touch.

"Your hand on me feels exquisite." He licked along her neck and laved the mark he'd given her then plunged two fingers deep inside her channel. He intended to love her however he could. He nipped her skin, dotting each and every inch under his mouth as he moved toward her breasts. Living a lifetime at her side was a dream he intended to make a reality, although clearly convincing her of the same would be a challenge, although one he was more than up for. "Cherub, tell me exactly what you want me to do."

"You're doing everything and more than I could ever ask for." She cupped his balls with one hand and with the other, she pumped his shaft. His spine tingled and a low burn hummed at the base of his spine, one that ricocheted around to the front and had him gritting his teeth to keep from coming.

"Damn it. I won't come before you." He drove his fingers into her and she whimpered and pushed her breasts against his chest.

"And I won't come afore you." She bit his neck and fire raced through his blood.

He exploded, his essence spurting from him in one fast burn. He coated her fingers and as he did, he sank his teeth into her neck and she cried out his name. Her inner core dragged his fingers in even deeper inside her and she came, over and over. He roared his pleasure. Never had he experienced such satisfaction as he had in this very moment, a satisfaction he intended to imbibe in again. Now, he just needed to convince his mate that he'd never accept another. Only her. He'd also never take her away from her duty but aid her in any and every way he could. She was his, if she was but willing to take a chance on him.

* * * *

Pure pleased raced through Cherub and she muffled her cries

against Kirk's neck. His cock pulsed in her hand just the same way as her inner channel pulsed around his fingers. When he'd slid his hand over her entrance and touched her very core, nothing had ever brought her such pleasure. He'd devoured her with his kisses and bites, as if he knew exactly what she needed and how to deliver it. Even now, he continued to slowly caress his fingers inside her as he gently brought them both back down.

She'd wanted this moment with him, just as desperately as he'd wanted it.

"Are you all right?" he whispered in her ear.

"Very." She cuddled into him and he wrapped his arms around her, his breaths coming slower until his beautiful golden eyes slowly slid shut and the long sweep of his eyelashes brushed his high cheeks. Long minutes passed. Quietly, she whispered his name, "Kirk?"

He didn't stir.

Well, it appeared she'd exhausted her mate. How interesting.

Smiling, she carefully straightened his clothing then hers. Goodness. She'd been so hungry for him, and although born in an era when a woman would never act so wantonly with a man, she was different. She hadn't remained in her true time for long before traveling the ages. And of late, she'd spent more time in the twenty-first century than here in the past. She was at home wherever her kin were, no matter the time or place.

With one finger, she touched her mate's lower lip. He held such a deep well of love within his heart and she could see why the fates had allowed their bond to take form. She'd adored each and every one of his kisses and even though she hadn't allowed a complete joining, in that moment when his seed had rushed forth from him and coated her fingers, she'd secretly wished his essence had instead spurted deep inside her.

More than a thousand years old and she'd never once been bedded. From the very beginning she'd chosen to remain alone, not once experiencing any desire to lie with a man. Those emotions had been a clear warning, that she would one day have a mate, that it would be just a matter of time before her soul became bound to another's. It was as Nessa had said. There was only one…for both of them.

Kirk's hold on her loosened as he fell deeper into sleep.

With a sigh, she wriggled free, her fingers so sticky. She'd wash up then wake him. Slippers kicked off and skirts scrunched high, she waded into the lapping surf and dunked her hands.

"Cherub?" Kirk groped the sand then scrambled to his feet, his wakefulness hitting him the moment she'd left his side.

"I'm right here, my tempting bear."

Eyes closed, he breathed deep and followed his nose toward her. "I can scent you."

"And what do I smell like?"

"You smell like sweet honey right now." He dropped to his knees in the water, clutched her waist and burrowed his nose into her belly. "It's completely intoxicating. I didn't mean to fall asleep. I was just so content and I've hardly gotten any rest of late. I've been too anxious as I awaited this night."

"You didnae offend me, so say no more about it." She buried her hands in his silky black locks as the surf splashed his pants and molded the black leather to his thighs. "You're getting wet."

"I care little about the water, only being close to you. My bear also wishes to meet you, actually he demands it." He rose, gripped the hem of his billowy white tunic, hauled it over his head and pitched it toward her cloak on the beach. He kicked off his boots then extended one arm. His skin rippled with fur as dark and as silky as the hair on his head, there one moment then gone the next.

"If you need to shift then do so. I'd like naught more than to see your other half, even as furry as he is."

"He might get a little possessive. He knows you're ours."

"There is naught you can do that will scare me, if that is your concern."

"I'll need to lose these pants so I can Change. Shredding my clothing is a pain in the butt and I prefer not to do it. Can you handle a little more nudity?"

"I believe I can." She licked her lips and near panted at the thought of seeing him fully unclothed. Oh dear, she was far more than just wanton. She was downright greedy. She stepped closer, stroked across his broad shoulders gleaming in the moonlight then traced one finger down the center of his wide chest and along the dusting of hair narrowing between his impressively hard abs and disappearing below the waistband of his pants. Only minutes ago she'd touched him below and doing so had brought her such pleasure. She swept her finger along his trim waist, back and forth as her desire to touch more of him flooded her once again.

Kirk caught her hand in his, his lips lifting. "My elusive imp, should you touch me again as you did just before, then I won't be held responsible for my actions. My cock is already trying to spear right through my pants for more of your exquisite attention."

"Then shift."

"As you wish." He shoved his pants down his heavily muscled legs, stepped out of them and tossed them aside. Under the moon's glow, he stood before her, so magnificently male and all hers.

Goodness, 'twas just as well he couldn't see how desperately she wanted him. Living more than a thousand years without any true companionship wasn't easy, and with him offering himself to her on a platter, the thought of leaving him was becoming more difficult by the minute. "Make the Change, Kirk." Husky words, which barely made it past her lips.

"Don't leave me while I'm in my other form." He fumbled to find her, grasped her face between his hands and brought her mouth to his for a searing kiss before he backed up and in a burst of brilliant lights, shifted and dropped to all fours. A big bear, his pelt a stunning midnight-black, lumbered toward her. He rose up on his hind legs and roared, his growl demanding all stayed far away from this place.

She swished through the lapping waves onto the sand and as she moved, he stalked her. She halted, held out one hand and he stuck his muzzle into her palm and licked her. Giggling, she knelt. "Your bear is beautiful, Kirk."

He rubbed the side of his body against her, almost knocking her over. She wrapped her arms around his neck to keep herself in place then stroked down his back and petted between his ears. When she stopped, he flopped down, rolled onto his back on the dry sand and exposed his belly.

"Do you wish for a tummy rub?"

One long rumble, which reverberated deep within his chest.

"That sounded like an aye to me." Hands spread over his belly, she stroked and as she did, he closed his eyes and fairly purred. There was naught more stunning to see than his bear. She laid down beside him and snuggled against his side. This was one of the most magical nights she'd ever had, and with her mate allowing her to see both sides of him, it made it even more special. Although what kind of a mate was she when she wouldn't even show him her true form?

"I'm sorry," she murmured in his ear. "You deserve so much more than to be bound to me, a woman who remains from your sight when you're fully prepared to show me all of you."

He growled and in a bright array of lights, swiftly made the Change then loomed over her, his dark hair falling forward over his brow as he narrowed his gaze on her chin.

"Look higher." She caught his face and directed his gaze to hers. "See, I hide from you. I'm sorry to cause you that pain."

"It's a pain I can bear, and you're only doing so in an attempt to protect me. The moment I have your image in my mind, it'll make our separation all the harder, whereas right now, I have only the knowledge you've shared. Blue eyes and blond hair. But I know exactly what counts, and that's what's on the inside and deep within your heart. You have such pure intentions and think only of others. You're all I could ever desire in a mate."

Tears misted her gaze and trickled free. She sniffed and he frowned.

"You're not crying are you?"

"Nay." She wiped the tears away but more rose and slid free.

"Damn it. You are. I can sense your lies." He traced across her cheeks and growled again when he encountered the wetness. "Please, don't cry. I never meant for my words to bring you any pain."

"They are good tears."

"No tears are good." He shoved to his feet and lifted her to hers. "What can I do to bring those giggles back?"

"Mayhap 'tis what I can do for you instead that will lighten my mood. Clothe yourself and I'll take you somewhere special." She stuck her slippers on, swung her cape over her shoulders and tied it in place.

He donned his clothes, boots and weapons, and she tried desperately not to sneak a long look at his deliciously hard body while he did.

Once he was dressed, she stepped up to him, wrapped her arms around his waist and settled her cheek on his wide chest. "I'm about to take you for a look at my world, and when I do, you'll experience a sense of weightlessness as we move through the sky. I'll also extend my cloaking to cover you. I can do so with others when needed."

"Wait." He shook his head. "I just realized. You must have been the one who opened the portal that brought me and my brothers through into this time. Isla too."

"I was. You never once thought it was me?" He'd said he'd heard the legend of the Fae Angel of Love.

"I didn't put the two together until right now. I didn't see you within the portal."

"Aye, just as you cannae see me in this moment."

"Right. The legend remains strong." He nodded. "Will this

experience be similar to that trip through the portal? There was a ton of wind swirling about and a whole lot of freefalling."

"I'm sorry that occurred, but it willnae this time. When one holds onto me while traveling through a portal, there is only the enjoyment of the flight. There will be no need for a portal though right now, just a pleasant night drifting through the sky. You will soar as I will, as if on the wings of a bird."

"Well, that sounds like the kind of ride I wouldn't want to miss out on."

"Then make sure you dinnae let go of me, otherwise there will most definitely be a whole lot of freefalling involved."

"Letting go of you right now will be impossible, not now that I've finally found you." He dipped his head, planted a kiss on her ear then groaned. "I was aiming for your mouth."

"My mouth is here." She lifted onto her toes and touched her lips to his. "Kiss me, Kirk, and we shall soar to the stars together."

"Mmm, and I only wish in more ways than one." He kissed her with a wild passion she couldn't help but respond to, and slowly, she lifted them higher and dipped and dived through the air, as in control of her element as she could be when he continually sent her thoughts awry.

Aye, the mated bond was a precious thing, and she only wished she never had to lay hers with him aside. Her mate was her match in every way, a man she could so easily fall in love with.

She bobbed over the village and drew in a deep breath. Below, smoke curled from several of the thatch-roofed houses and wisped into the night sky. Children dashed about the cottages, barefoot as they played tag, their squeals reaching her and tugging at her heart. Around a fire pit in the center of the village, both young and old chatted. Her people would always need her, just as she'd always need them. She wasn't just a time-walker but their princess. That she could never forget.

One night. She'd continue to enjoy this one night, cherish and hold it tight.

That she could do.

The Matheson Brothers

Highlander's Desire, Book One
Highlander's Passion, Book Two
Highlander's Seduction, Book Three

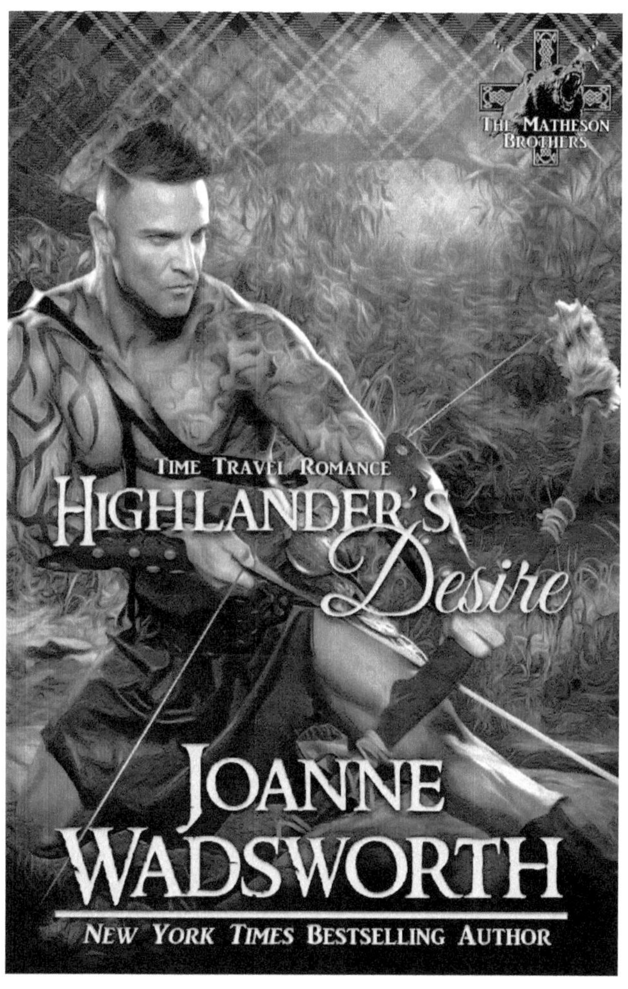

The Matheson Brothers Continued

Highlander's Bride, Book Seven
Highlander's Caress, Book Eight
Highlander's Touch, Book Nine

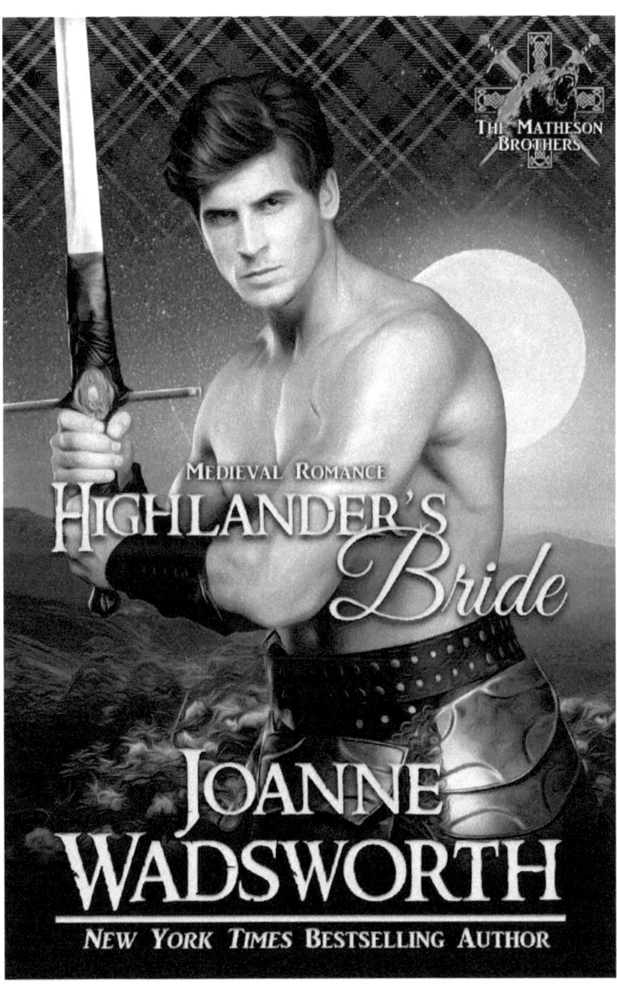

The Matheson Brothers Continued

Highlander's Shifter, Book Ten
Highlander's Claim, Book Eleven
Highlander's Courage, Book Twelve
Highlander's Mermaid, Book Thirteen

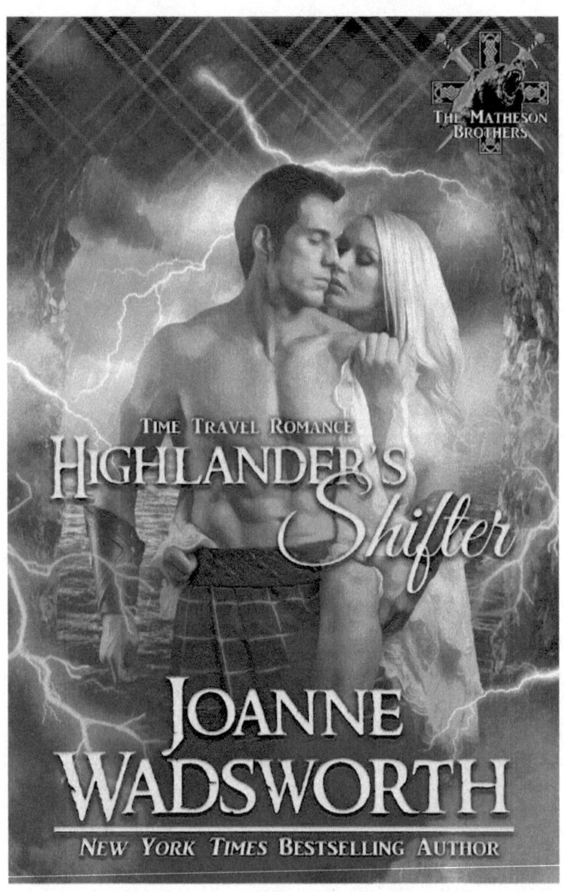

Highlander Heat

Highlander's Castle, Book One
Highlander's Magic, Book Two
Highlander's Charm, Book Three
Highlander's Guardian, Book Four
Highlander's Faerie, Book Five
Highlander's Champion, Book Six

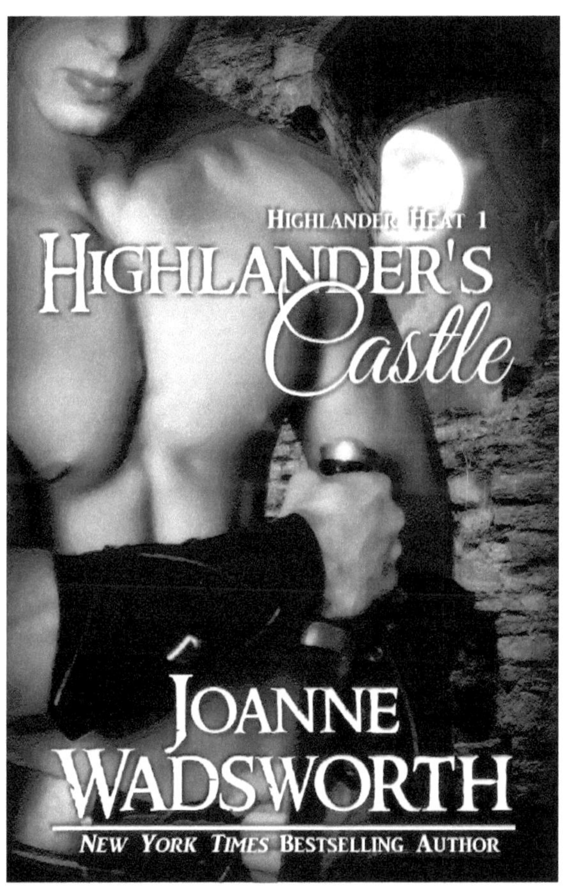

Regency Brides

The Duke's Bride, Book One
The Earl's Bride, Book Two
The Wartime Bride, Book Three
The Earl's Secret Bride, Book Four
The Prince's Bride, Book Five
Her Pirate Prince, Book Six

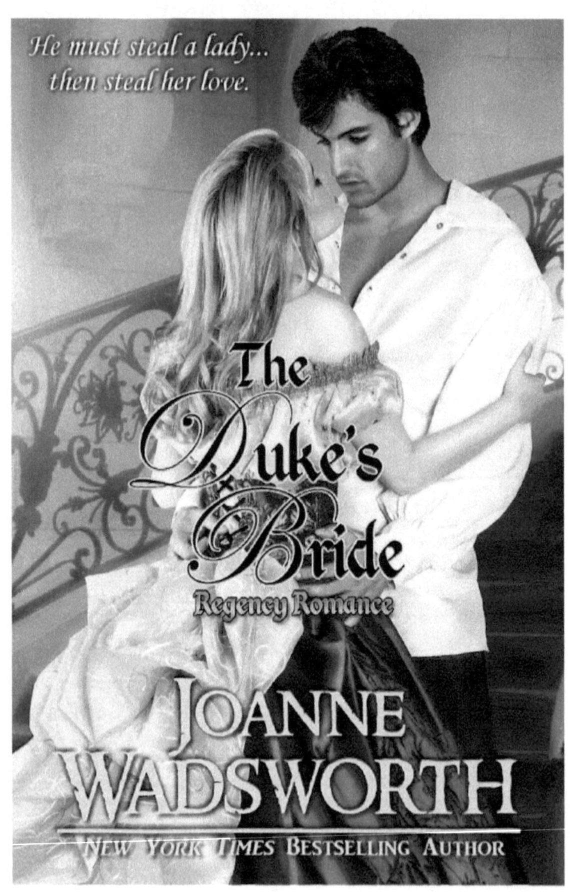

Princesses of Myth

Protector, Book One
Warrior, Book Two
Hunter (Short Story - Included in Warrior, Book Two)
Enchanter, Book Three
Healer, Book Four
Chaser, Book Five

Billionaire Bodyguards

Billionaire Bodyguard Attraction, Book One
Billionaire Bodyguard Boss, Book Two
Billionaire Bodyguard Fling, Book Three

JOANNE WADSWORTH

Joanne Wadsworth is a *New York Times* and *USA Today* Bestselling Author who adores getting lost in the world of romance, no matter what era in time that might be. Hot alpha Highlanders hound her, demanding their stories are told and she's devoted to ensuring they meet their match, whether that be with a feisty lass from the present or far in the past.

Living on a tiny island at the bottom of the world, she calls New Zealand home. Big-dreamer, hoarder of chocolate, and addicted to juicy watermelons since the age of five, she chases after her four energetic children and has her own hunky hubby on the side.

So come and join in all the fun, because this kiwi girl promises to give you her "Hot-Highlander" oath, to bring you a heart-pounding, sexy adventure from the moment you turn the first page. This is where romance meets fantasy and adventure…

To learn more about Joanne and her works, visit
http://www.joannewadsworth.com